A CHANGE OF HEART

As Danielle began warming up, she realized she didn't feel the same excitement that the others seemed to feel. All she could think about was how much she had to do between now and the competition. How hard she would have to work. She began skating her routine, hoping to lose herself in her skating the way she used to. Suddenly she remembered her short story. A thrill of happiness washed over her.

"Aren't you excited, Dani?" Tori asked when they took a break by the railing.

"I really am," Danielle answered. "Did Nikki tell you?"

"Nikki? No, Kathy announced it this morning," Tori said.

"Oh, you mean about the competition," Danielle said.

Tori gave her a strange look. "Of course. What did you think I meant?"

"I thought—oh, never mind." Tori would never understand. Danielle doubted the others would either. If she told them she was more excited about a short story contest than about the next skating competition, they would think she was crazy.

She looked at her watch and sighed. What was wrong with her? Practice had just started, and here she was counting the minutes until it was over.

A
SURPRISE
TWIST

Melissa Lowell

Created by Parachute Press

A SKYLARK BOOK
NEW YORK · TORONTO · LONDON · SYDNEY · AUCKLAND

RL 5, IL ages 9–12

A SURPRISE TWIST
A Skylark Book / September 1995

Skylark Books is a registered trademark of Bantam Books, a division of Bantam Doubleday Dell Publishing Group, Inc. Registered in the U.S. Patent and Trademark Office and elsewhere.

Series design: Barbara Berger

ISBN 0-553-48317-X

Published simultaneously in the United States and Canada

Bantam Books are published by Bantam Books, a division of Bantam Doubleday Dell Publishing Group, Inc. Its trademark, consisting of the words "Bantam Books" and the portrayal of a rooster, is Registered in the U.S. Patent and Trademark Office and in other countries. Marca Registrada. Bantam Books, 1540 Broadway, New York, New York 10036.

PRINTED IN THE UNITED STATES OF AMERICA

CWO   0   9   8   7   6   5   4   3   2   1

1

As Danielle Panati and Nikki Simon hurried down the hall to find their lockers, Danielle felt a sudden thrill of excitement. Usually she dreaded the first day back to school after summer vacation. But this year things were going to be different. It was going to be a good year.

"I hope we have some classes together," Danielle said.

"Me too," Nikki said. "I'd never have made it through math last year without you." She reached up to pat Danielle playfully on the shoulder. Last year Nikki and Danielle had been almost the same height, but since Danielle's growth spurt, Nikki was much shorter.

"Danielle! Nikki!" someone called from down the hall.

Danielle spun around and saw Kara Logan rushing toward them. Danielle smiled. Kara was always rushing. She was into a million different things. She had tons of friends and was totally boy-crazy. At the end of last year she had had a crush on a boy named Steve Kedder.

"Is Kara still dating Steve?" Danielle asked Nikki.

"Are you kidding?" Nikki's grin showed her braces. "You know Kara. If she stays with a guy for a week it's a record."

"Have you found your lockers yet?" Kara asked when she caught up to them. She flipped her blond hair over her shoulder. "Mine's right here." She yanked open her locker door and stashed her lunch bag inside. "Whew," she said, wrinkling her nose. "It smells like someone left a pair of dirty socks in it all summer. I hope they fumigated them."

Kara slammed her locker shut and turned back to Danielle and Nikki. "Danielle! Look at you," Kara cried, staring at Danielle in amazement. "You're so lucky! Nikki told me about your growth spurt. How tall are you now?" She held up her hand to measure herself against Danielle. "We used to be the same height and now look. I come up to your nose." She stood back and studied Danielle. "You look fabulous!"

Danielle knew she had changed a lot. She had shot up to five foot seven over the summer. Her mother and her grandmother had been driving her crazy talking about it all the time. Dani had been average height and a little on the plump side. But now, all of a sudden, she was tall and thin. Her new height had taken some getting used to, but she had to admit, she liked her new look.

"Isn't it great?" Nikki said. "You should see the guys at the ice rink, they absolutely drool over her. It's disgusting."

Nikki and Danielle were both members of Silver Blades, one of the top skating clubs in the country. They had been practicing together all summer, and now that school had started they would skate every morning before school, and again in the afternoon. It was a grueling schedule. But to them, and to the other Silver Blades skaters, it was worth it.

Nikki and Danielle found their lockers. Danielle opened her backpack and took out her binder and her schedule. "What do you have first period?" she asked Nikki.

Nikki checked her schedule. "Math. Room 202. With Mr. Justin. Ugh! He's supposed to be a slave driver. How about you, Dani?"

"History, Room 208. Mr. Parsons. I don't know much about him."

The bell rang, and the girls grabbed their books and started in opposite directions down the hall. As Danielle headed for her history class, she saw her brother Nicholas and two other guys walking toward her. She recognized one of them, Chase Cameron. The other one was unfamiliar. As they came closer, Danielle heard Chase say, "Isn't that your sister, Panati? The one you used to call Tubs? She doesn't look like a tub to me!"

Danielle straightened up, trying to look cool and casual as they came closer. But instead of giving them a sophisticated wave and smile as she had planned, she tripped right in front of them. Her binder went flying, and papers scattered everywhere.

"Yeah, that's my sister, all right," Nicholas said, laughing. "I don't call her Tubs anymore, though. Now I call her Klutz."

Danielle could feel her face turning purple with embarrassment. She scrambled to pick up her things. Why did she have to trip right in front of them?

She was trying to ignore her brother and Chase when the other boy, the one she didn't know, stooped down to help her.

"You're Nicholas's sister?" he asked, gathering up her spilled papers.

"So my parents say. Personally I think there was a mistake at the hospital. He was obviously switched at birth with a child from hell," Danielle said.

The boy laughed. "I just met him a few days ago

at Chase's. I'm Zack, by the way. Zack Hutton." He handed her some more papers.

"I'm Danielle. Thanks, Zack."

The late bell rang, and Danielle started off down the hall.

"See you around," Zack called after her.

"Okay," she called back, surprised. Nicholas and his friend were in ninth grade. Most of them didn't pay much attention to Danielle—except to tease her the way Nicholas did. She had had a major crush on one of his friends last year. A hockey player named Jordan McShane. Danielle remembered how she'd thought he was the coolest guy in school. When he'd finally noticed her, she'd been totally thrilled. They had hung out together a lot the second half of the year. But when summer came Jordan went away, and she hadn't heard from him once. She was still angry that he hadn't answered any of her letters. Maybe Zack was different, she thought. Anyway, he was cute, and at least he was friendly.

Why had she tripped right in front of them? She really had been a klutz lately. She guessed it had something to do with her new height. It wouldn't matter so much, except that as an ice-skater she was supposed to be graceful. Lately she felt anything but graceful. She even felt clumsy on the ice, and she had to admit it was beginning to affect her skating.

Like at that morning's practice. She'd been working on a double salchow. She had landed the jump in the summer, but lately, even though she tried again and again, she couldn't get the height she needed to finish the second rotation. It was frustrating, but she knew if she kept working she'd get it. As her coach, Mr. Weiler, was always telling her, perseverance—not giving up—that's what competitive skating was all about.

Danielle raced to history class and slid into her seat just in time. Mr. Parsons spent most of the period telling them about all the work he expected from them. When the class ended everyone was talking about how hard it was going to be.

"My sister had him two years ago," said a girl named Sharon Naylor. "She almost had a nervous breakdown."

Great, thought Danielle. Just what I need, extra work. Maybe her other classes would be easier.

What's next? Danielle wondered, pulling out her schedule. English, Room 106. Ms. Howard. Honors. *Honors*? They put me in honors English? That was for the brains, Danielle thought. The kids who had their noses in their books from morning till night. It was the last thing she needed.

Looking around the classroom, Danielle was positive it was going to be a disaster. Only the really smart kids were there. And then there's me, she thought. She found a seat in the back of the room, hoping she wouldn't be noticed.

But as the class got under way, Danielle found herself enjoying it. The teacher, Ms. Howard, was young and seemed pretty cool. Danielle liked the way she talked to the kids. She seemed truly interested in what they had to say. Danielle surprised herself by raising her hand and joining in the discussion. Actually, when she thought about it, she realized she had always done pretty well in English. It was one of her favorite subjects, so maybe this class wouldn't be a total disaster after all.

At lunch Danielle sat with Nikki and Jill Wong, another Silver Blades friend. The three of them had been best friends for years, along with two other Silver Blades skaters, Tori Carsen and Haley Arthur. Tori and Haley both went to a private school, Kent Academy, in nearby Burgess. Danielle, Nikki, and Jill were Grandview Middle School's only skaters. Danielle couldn't imagine life without them all.

"You're taking honors English?" Jill exclaimed when she heard. "Wow. You're going to have to work. Those guys practically study twenty-four hours a day."

"I know. It's going to be hard. But the teacher's cool. I really like her." Danielle unwrapped her sandwich and took a bite.

"Yeah," said Nikki. "Teachers are always cool on the first day back. They want to fool you into thinking they're human. Just wait."

Danielle laughed. "Well, my history teacher didn't even bother to pretend. He spent the whole period telling us how hard we were going to be working."

"Well, at least you don't have science right before lunch. We're studying the human digestive tract. It's so disgusting. I'm never going to feel like eating after that class," said Jill.

The rest of the day passed quickly. But when it was over, Danielle felt drained. She almost wished she didn't have to go to skating practice. But, she told herself, it would be good to get on the ice and just skate. It always helped to work out the tension of the first day back.

At the rink Danielle changed into her black leggings and a bright multicolored sweater that she had just gotten. She had outgrown almost all of her old clothes and had had to buy a lot of new things. Getting to buy new clothes was one of the great things about having a growth spurt, Danielle thought, although her mother hadn't been too happy about spending all that money.

She glanced at herself in the mirror as she left the locker room. She loved the way her new sweater looked.

As Danielle stretched she saw Nikki with Tori and Haley already out on the ice. She hurried to catch up with them, dying to hear about their first day back at Kent. She hit the ice, joining the other three girls. The four of them skated around the rink, warming up and talking excitedly.

"You should see Mr. Martin, our history teacher," Tori told Danielle. "He looks exactly like Patrick Swayze." Tori's cobalt-blue skating outfit looked great with her blue eyes and curly blond hair.

"And he's funny," Haley added. Haley had red hair and huge brown eyes, and wore an earring in one ear. When anyone asked Haley why she wore only one earring, she said it was because when she'd gone to get her ears pierced, the first one hurt so much she decided not to get the other one done. But Danielle knew it was really because Haley liked to be different. She was kind of a tomboy, and she definitely had her own style.

"He even laughed at your fake chalk trick," Tori said.

"Yeah. He's definitely cool," said Haley.

"Don't tell me Haley has struck already." Danielle laughed. Haley was known for her practical jokes.

"Well, he's new," Haley explained. "We have to break these new teachers in right away. All I did was switch the regular chalk with this chalk that crumbles the minute you try to write with it. It took him a while to catch on. It was pretty funny."

"You're lucky Mr. Martin has a good sense of humor," Tori told her.

"Tomorrow he gets the rubber pencil." Haley gave them her evil grin, wiggling her eyebrows.

Danielle laughed. "I wish you were in my math class. Ms. Saunders is incredibly boring. She has this monotone voice and she drones on and on. The whole class was practically asleep by the end of the period. We need you to liven things up."

"I could lend you something from my bag of tricks," Haley suggested.

"No." Danielle shook her head. "Without you it wouldn't be the same. If I tried playing a trick it would backfire. Something awful would happen, and I'd end up with thirty days of detention."

All too soon, warm-up time was over. Danielle wished they could spend the whole time skating and talking. But their coaches, Kathy Bart and Franz Weiler, were signaling that it was time to get to work. The four of them broke up.

Danielle chose a spot on the ice where she could concentrate on the double salchow. But it went just the way it had that morning. She tried it again and again, but still couldn't manage to finish the second rotation.

"Height, Danielle. Height," Mr. Weiler called

from the center of the rink. She knew he was watching, and somehow that made it worse. It was so frustrating. She had done this jump before. Why couldn't she get it now?

She struggled for another half hour. Finally, in frustration, she rotated her shoulders way too much and landed on her backside. Mr. Weiler skated over and offered her a hand.

"You have grown so much this summer," he said.

Danielle nodded.

"Your new growth is the problem. Your muscles have not caught up with you," Mr. Weiler went on. "You're having trouble lifting yourself up to get the height you need."

That made sense, Danielle thought. Something was wrong, that much she knew.

"Why don't we start you on a special program of weight training? That will strengthen your leg muscles. Talk to Ernie in the weight room. See when he can fit you in."

"Okay," Danielle said. She knew he was right. If her legs were stronger, she would be able to get the height she needed for her jumps. But a weight training program was the last thing she wanted right now. How was she ever going to fit it in? And besides, she hated weight training.

Nikki and Tori were already taking off their skates. Danielle slumped onto the bench beside them and began unlacing her own skates. "Weight training," she groaned. "I hate weight training."

"It's the price you pay for growing," Tori said.

"I think you're lucky," Nikki said. "I wish I had a body like yours."

Danielle had to admit she loved being tall and thin. If only it hadn't affected her jumps.

They headed for the locker room. "Tori," Nikki said, "you've really got that double axel down. You look great."

"Thanks. I plan to use it in my program for the next competition. I hope I'm ready."

"You definitely are," Nikki told her.

"You and Alex looked good, too," Haley commented. "Are you working on something new?"

Nikki and Haley skated pairs. Nikki's partner was Alex Beekman, an eighth-grader at Kent. Haley skated with Patrick McGuire, who looked so much like her that everyone thought they were brother and sister.

"We've been working on the death spiral and the split double twist," Nikki said, naming two advanced and somewhat risky moves. "How about you?"

The three girls chatted away.

Everyone's working on new things, Danielle thought. Everyone but me. I can't even master the same old jumps I could do at the beginning of the summer. It's too depressing.

But in the locker room, she caught sight of herself in the mirror. For a minute she almost didn't recognize herself. She was tall. Tall and thin. She had been aware, of course, that she had grown a lot over the summer, but she still couldn't believe how different she looked. She swept her hair back and struck a pose for the mirror. She looked elegant, and . . . and beautiful. She remembered the way Zack had looked at her that morning. If boys like Zack were starting to notice the new Danielle, she didn't care how hard she had to work on her double salchow!

2

In English class the following day, Danielle surprised herself by choosing a seat near the front of the room. She always used to sit at the back so that she wouldn't be called on much. Maybe Nikki was right and teachers were only nice on the first day, but Danielle was pretty sure Ms. Howard would stay cool. Anyway, she sure had great clothes. Today she had on a long, straight skirt with a slit on the side, a cream-colored blouse, and a black suede vest. Her curly brown hair was gathered into a loose ponytail.

"Let's talk about *A Tree Grows in Brooklyn*," Ms. Howard said, holding up her copy of the book. It was one they had been assigned to read over the summer. "First of all, how'd you like it?"

"It was good," someone said, and Danielle nodded in agreement. She had genuinely enjoyed reading it.

"Booor-ing," said James Jarman, one of the biggest brains in the middle school.

"Danielle, I see you nodding. Does that mean you liked it or you thought it was booor-ing, like James?"

"I liked it," Danielle said, a little embarrassed.

"Can you tell us why? Anything in particular that you liked?"

Danielle frowned, struggling to put her thoughts into words. Her heart was pounding as she spoke. "Well, I felt like even though it takes place a long time ago, I could really identify with Francie and a lot of what she was going through."

"That's something we all look for in a good book—a character we can understand and identify with," said Ms. Howard.

"You could identify with that geek?" James said. "I couldn't."

"But things were different back then," Danielle went on. She couldn't believe she was disagreeing with James Jarman. She was sure she'd end up looking like a fool, but she continued anyway. "I mean, Francie had to really struggle for everything she got. But the way she felt about things, like her family, and hoping the tree would grow, those feelings weren't geeky. And that's what I could identify with."

Ms. Howard nodded. "An insightful answer, Danielle. You put your finger on exactly why we read fiction. Exactly why we still love Shakespeare, and Jane Austen, and books that were written hundreds of years ago in different times and places. Because human emotion really doesn't change, does it? James, how do you respond to what Danielle says?"

"Well, I guess I see what she means, but as a guy I had a hard time relating."

"So you're saying it's a girl's book? What do the rest of you think?"

As they went on discussing the book, Danielle forgot to be scared. She was surprised at herself. Last year she would have been way too shy to contribute, but this year she enjoyed it. She really had changed. Once she had wanted to hide. Now she wanted to be heard.

It seemed as though class had just begun when Ms. Howard checked her watch and said, "Well, I'm afraid that's all we have time for today."

Danielle couldn't believe it. The class had flown by. "I hope we can continue this discussion tomorrow," Ms. Howard went on. "I heard some thoughtful and interesting ideas expressed here today. Thank you all." Was it Danielle's imagination, or did the teacher seem to be smiling right at her as she complimented them?

As Danielle left the classroom a girl named Megan McCord fell into step beside her. "She's a cool teacher, isn't she?" Megan commented. Megan was small and had a cloud of reddish gold hair that fell below her shoulders in soft waves. With her clear white skin and tiny, well-defined features, she reminded Danielle of an elf. She wore round gold-rimmed glasses, which she never took off. Danielle had had classes with Megan before, but had never really gotten to know her.

"She's great," Danielle answered. "She gets everyone talking."

"Sounds like you really liked *A Tree Grows in Brooklyn*," Megan said as they walked down the hall.

"I did," Danielle said. "It was definitely the best book I read this summer." Then she was afraid she would sound like a geek who loved school, so she added, "But I absolutely hated the one we had to read for history, the one about the French Revolution."

"Me too!" Megan cried. "Wasn't that the most boring thing in the world? The minute I looked at it I fell asleep."

"Same," Danielle said with a laugh. Megan's really nice, she thought. She was surprised because she had always assumed that Megan was kind of snobby, someone who would never bother speaking to her. But she wasn't like that at all, Danielle realized.

"You should read this." Megan held out a book. "It's by the same author as *A Tree Grows in Brooklyn*, but even better. You can borrow it if you want."

"Thanks," Danielle said. She knew she probably wouldn't have time to read the book, but she was flattered that Megan had taken the time to give it to her.

As if she could read her mind, Megan said, "I guess it's hard to find time to read with your skating and all, huh?"

"Skating really does take up a lot of my time," Danielle said with a sigh. She was pleased that Megan knew she skated.

"It must be hard, getting up so early every morning." Megan said. "I hear you're fantastic, though. Everyone says you'll probably make it to the Olympics someday."

"Ha. I wish. Right now I'll just be happy to qualify for Regionals."

"Where do you skate? I'd love to watch you sometime."

"At the Seneca Hills Ice Arena. It's not far."

"Yeah, I know where that is. My little brother plays ice hockey there."

"Hey, why don't you meet me there on Saturday? We could do something afterwards. Sometimes we all go to a movie or the mall or something," Danielle suggested.

"Cool. I'd love that. I'll ask my Mom and let you know tomorrow," Megan answered.

"Great!"

"Well, see you." Megan gave Danielle a friendly wave as she hurried down the hall.

Megan's cool, Danielle thought as she hurried to her next class. Making a new friend made Danielle feel good for the rest of the day.

That afternoon at the rink, Danielle was rushing to get to the locker room to change for afternoon practice. Mr. Weiler had told her he wanted her to have an extra lesson during practice that afternoon, so that they could work on getting height in her jumps. She wasn't watching where she was going as she rounded the corner, and she bumped smack into Jordan McShane, the boy she had liked so much all last year.

Danielle's skating bag dropped and flew open.

"Danielle!" Jordan exclaimed. "I—I'm sorry. Didn't mean to run you down. Here, let me help."

Danielle was so flustered, she could hardly speak. She hadn't seen Jordan since the beginning of the summer, and it still hurt that she hadn't heard from him either, even though she had written him. She bent down to pick up her stuff, and he knelt down to help.

"Hey, you . . . you look great," Jordan said. "Have you grown or something?"

"Yeah, I guess so," Danielle said.

"How was your summer?" Jordan asked.

"Good, thanks." The creep, Danielle thought. How could he ask about her summer? If he had really wanted to know, he could have called or written her.

"Listen, Danielle, I'm sorry I never answered your letters. I really wanted to write you . . . but I'm not that good at writing letters. I thought about you a lot, though."

Yeah, sure, Danielle thought. But she said, "Oh, that's okay. I didn't really expect you to answer."

She straightened up and closed her bag. Jordan kept on staring at her. "Wow. You look so different. I can't get over it," he said.

"Yeah, well, I have to go."

"Danielle, wait. . . . Would you like to go to a movie sometime?"

Danielle stared at him as a million different feelings rushed through her. Last year she had liked him so much! She remembered how excited she'd been when he'd first asked her out. But she had felt so shy on their only real date that she had hardly spoken. Then, over the summer, she was so hurt and angry when he didn't write. And now here he was, asking her out again. What should she do? Did she really want to go out with him?

"Umm, maybe, but I'm kind of busy this year," she answered.

"I'll call you, okay?"

"Yeah, okay." Danielle rushed to the girls' locker room before he could say anything more. She looked at her watch. She was late! She changed quickly and hurried out to the rink, hoping maybe Mr. Weiler would be late, too. Sometimes he got held up. But as she laced her skates she saw him already on the ice, skating back and forth and checking his watch impatiently.

"You are late, Danielle," he said as she skated toward him.

"I'm sorry, I—I just got held up."

"Yes, well, try to be on time. I had enough trouble trying to fit you in for an extra lesson. But we are here now, so let's begin. Let me see your salchow."

Good, thought Danielle. She knew she could do a perfect salchow. The jump required timing and balance, but not too much height. She stroked counterclockwise around the rink, went into an inside Mohawk, and lifted off her left back inside edge, rotating her arms and shoulders counterclockwise to make one revolution. Then she landed on her right back inside edge.

"Excellent. Now let's see a double Lutz."

Danielle had landed a double Lutz once last spring, but so far that was the only time. Lately she hadn't even been close to landing it again.

She skated back crossovers, shifted her weight to her left foot, placed her right toe pick in the ice and sprang into the air from her left leg. She rotated her shoulders counterclockwise and looked over her left shoulder. The liftoff felt good, but she didn't get enough height. She landed leaning forward and off balance.

"Height, height, height!" Mr. Weiler cried. "Try it again."

Danielle tried again and again, but each time she failed to get the height she needed to complete two full rotations. By the end of her lesson, she was so frustrated she felt close to tears. She had landed this jump before. Why couldn't she get it now? She felt as if she were going backward while the rest of the skaters were progressing. She tried once more, but in her frustration she overrotated and landed on her backside.

"Okay, Danielle. That's enough for today. How is the weight training going?"

Danielle didn't know what to say. She hadn't begun the program yet. She hadn't even talked to Ernie about it.

"I, uh, I haven't had a chance to . . ."

Frowning, Mr. Weiler said, "Danielle, it is most important that you strengthen your leg muscles. And the weight program will help you feel more comfortable with your new height. Don't be discouraged. Many athletes go through a period of awkwardness when they experience a growth spurt. It's very common. But it does take some extra effort to work through it. I know you can do it if you want to. Why don't you go talk to Ernie right now? He can help you."

Danielle was glad her lesson was over and glad to be getting off the ice. She felt as if she hadn't done anything right. She felt like a beginner again. It was so frustrating, she almost wished she hadn't had a growth spurt.

But as she sat down to take off her skates she remembered all the good things that had happened in school. The way she had spoken up in English, and the compliments she had gotten from Ms. Howard. And making friends with Megan McCord. Except for skating, it had been a good day.

As she unlaced her skates, Nikki slid onto the bench beside her. Danielle couldn't wait to tell her about Jordan.

"Guess who saw I right before practice?" Danielle asked.

"Who?" Nikki answered.

"Jordan McShane!"

"You're kidding." Nikki frowned. "That creep. Did he talk to you?"

"Yeah, and I almost knocked him over. By mistake. But then he helped me pick up my stuff."

"After the way he treated you this summer, I'm surprised you *didn't* knock him over," Nikki said.

"Actually, he was pretty nice. He apologized for

not writing. And then he asked if I wanted to go out sometime."

"You're kidding? What did you say?"

"I said I didn't know."

"Do you like him again?" Nikki asked.

"I don't know. I'm so confused," Danielle said. "I feel like there's so much going on in my life right now."

Nikki put her arm around Danielle. "Don't worry. It's probably 'cause school just started. It's always hard to get back into the routine. Things will calm down soon."

"You're right. Anyway, I'm not going to let Jordan McShane worry me anymore. I did enough worrying about him this summer."

"Right. And besides, there are plenty of other guys out there," Nikki said.

As they headed for the locker room, Danielle decided Nikki was right. She was feeling overwhelmed because it was only the first week back at school. Soon enough she'd be back into the boring old routine.

3

In history class the following Monday, Danielle was trying to pay attention, but she couldn't concentrate on anything the teacher said. She couldn't wait until next period, when she would get her first English paper back from Ms. Howard. She had worked hard on it, but she had no idea what kind of grade she would get. Someone had told her that Ms. Howard was a really hard grader.

Danielle watched the second hand make its way slowly around the clock. Only six more minutes, she told herself. She wasn't exactly sure why this grade was so important to her. But she really liked Ms. Howard, and she wanted the teacher to think she was a good writer. Anyway, whatever the reason, it mattered, and she was nervous.

Finally the bell rang. Danielle gathered up her things and hurried to English.

When she got to class, Megan was already there. Megan had come by the rink on Saturday and watched Danielle skate, and then they had gone to the mall along with Danielle's Silver Blades friends.

"Danielle, over here," Megan called. "I saved you a seat."

"Thanks." Danielle slid into the desk next to Megan's. "I'm so nervous. I hope I did well on this paper."

"Me too. I really worked hard on it."

Danielle held her breath as Ms. Howard passed back the papers. Megan was one of the first to get hers. She turned it over and Danielle heard her whisper, "Yes," when she saw the grade.

Danielle looked over and Megan proudly showed her the A2 .

"Wow! That's great. You're so lucky."

Ms. Howard placed Danielle's paper on her desk. "Nice work, Danielle," she said.

Danielle turned the paper over and saw a big red A in the corner. Next to it Ms. Howard had written, "Excellent. You have presented a thoughtful, original argument in a clear and concise style."

"I knew it," Megan said when she saw Danielle's grade. "I knew you'd get an A. Hey, can I read it?"

"Sure," Danielle said. She passed the paper to Megan. An A, thought Danielle. She had gotten plenty of A's before, but this one really meant a lot to her.

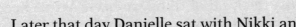

Later that day Danielle sat with Nikki and Jill at their usual lunch table.

"So, in a few more weeks I should be back on the ice," Jill was saying.

"That's so great. I bet you can't wait," Danielle said. "You must be sick of all that physical therapy you've been doing."

Jill nodded and was about to reply when Megan rushed up to their table.

"Danielle, I've got to talk to you." She sat down in an empty chair. "Hi, Jill. Hi, Nikki. Sorry for barging in, but this is so exciting! I can't wait to tell Dani."

"Tell me what?" Danielle asked.

"Well, you know I'm the features editor for the student paper, right?"

"Right."

"And our next issue is a special sports issue. And you are the perfect person to contribute an article. I already talked to Ms. Howard about it. She's our adviser, and she agrees—you're perfect."

"Why me? I've never written anything for the paper," Danielle said.

"That doesn't matter," Megan said. "You're a fantastic writer. I read your English paper, remember? It was terrific. Plus you've got an inside angle on what's it's like to be a competitive skater. That's just the kind of thing we need. We've been looking for athletes who can write."

Megan opened a container of yogurt, ate a spoonful, and then went on. "See, that's one reason I wanted to come and watch you skate the other day. I was thinking of maybe doing an interview with you or something. But now that I know you can write, I think it would be much better if *you* did an article for us."

"Look, just because I got an A on one English paper, that doesn't mean I can write an article," Danielle said.

"True. That's why I asked Ms. Howard what she thought. And she thinks you're really talented."

"Ms. Howard said that?" Danielle asked.

"She did. You've got to do it."

"I don't know," Danielle said. "I'm so busy with skating."

"Look, it's just one article. You don't have to join the newspaper staff. If it's too much work, well, there's no commitment."

Danielle thought about how much she liked to write. It would be fun to have an article in the paper. She wanted to do it, but where would she find the time?

"What kind of article would it be exactly?" she asked.

"Well, it has to be about competitive skating, of course. But beyond that, it's up to you. You could do a personal experience piece about what it's like to skate competitively. Or you could interview other skaters. . . . "

"I don't know if I'd like to write about myself," Danielle said. "But interviewing other skaters would be fun."

"You could interview me," said Nikki.

"And me," said Jill.

"We really need you," Megan coaxed. "And wouldn't you love to see your name in print?"

"Well . . ." Danielle hesitated. "I would like to give it a try. Okay, I'll do it."

"Great!" Megan put out her hand, and Danielle slapped it. "You have plenty of time. We don't need final copy until a week from today."

"A week! That's all?" Danielle cried.

"Hey. That's a long time. Usually our articles are due yesterday. A week is plenty of time. Don't worry. You'll do a great job."

Before Danielle could change her mind, Megan was gone, hurrying to talk to someone at another table.

"We'll be in the paper," Nikki said. "This is going to be so cool!"

"I can't believe I let her talk me into doing this article. How am I going to get it done?"

"You'll manage," Nikki told her. "I think it's great."

As Danielle finished her sandwich, she began to plan the article in her head.

"Come on," Nikki said. "We'd better hurry. If I'm late for math again, Mr. Massy will give me one of his looks. I can't take any more of his looks."

Jill laughed. "I know. He acts like coming late to class is worse than robbing a bank."

Danielle popped the rest of her granola bar into her mouth and picked up her tray. "Let's go," she said. "I've got study hall. I think I'll get started on the article. When can I interview you guys?"

Nikki and Jill took out their schedules, and they set up a time for the interviews.

Danielle was excited. The article was already beginning to take shape in her mind. First she would interview the members of Silver Blades. She'd use a sample of skaters, too, not just her own friends. She'd interview beginners and more advanced skaters. She'd interview the kids who'd never been in a competition and kids who'd already won medals at big, important competitions across the country.

Why, she could even insert a sort of champion piece—a second article that went along with the interviews. That article could have pictures and information about some of her skating idols. Skaters like Nancy Kerrigan, Oksana Baiul, Elvis Stojko . . .

Now Danielle was really getting excited. If Megan and the others on the paper went for the idea, it would be fantastic! She could see it now—"Skating Stars of Today" would be the title of the article about her favorite skaters. And "Skating Stars of Tomorrow" would be the title of the article with her interviews!

She thought about it the rest of the day and that afternoon at the rink while she was warming up with Nikki, Tori, and Haley.

"My mom was talking about how much you've grown," Tori told Danielle.

"She was?"

"She said it will probably be good for your career. She has this theory that tall skaters get noticed more than short ones."

Nikki looked puzzled. "That doesn't make sense. Look at Oksana Baiul. She's tiny."

"Since when do Mrs. Carsen's theories make sense?" Haley commented. "She also has a theory that the louder she yells, the better Tori will skate."

Tori's mother was known for pushing Tori really hard.

"Not so much anymore," Tori said. "Ever since she met Roger, she doesn't pay as much attention to me."

"You ought to be thankful he came along," Haley said.

"Yeah, I guess so. Except she's hardly ever around anymore. I have to do everything for myself. It's not that easy. Especially with all the work we have this year. I don't know about Grandview, but Kent is a lot harder in the eighth grade. Don't you think so, Haley?"

"Did you forget? I'm just a seventh-grader! But I have to say this year is much harder for me, too. I've got homework in every single class every night. These teachers all think their class is the only one we're taking."

"I know. It's like they forget we might have something to do besides homework," Tori complained. "How about Grandview? Is it hard this year?"

"I've had tons more work. Haven't you, Dani?" Nikki asked.

"Yeah, but I like it better this year. I guess my teachers are more interesting or something."

"Dani's writing an article for the newspaper," Nikki told Tori and Haley. "She's going to interview me and Jill."

"Cool. Can I be in it, too?" asked Tori.

"I think I need to stick to the kids who go to Grandview," Danielle explained.

"Oh," Tori said, sounding disappointed. "So how come you're writing an article? Is it an English assignment or something?"

"No. Megan McCord asked me to do it. She works on the newspaper. And I thought it would be fun."

"Fun?" Tori said. "Sounds like work to me. And I've got plenty of that. When will you have time for it between skating and school?"

"I don't know. But I'll fit it in. Don't you ever feel like you want to try something else? Something besides skating, I mean?"

"Sometimes. But I know I can't. Skating takes up too much time," Nikki said.

Tori shook her head. "Personally, I think writing for the newspaper sounds like a big bore."

"But what about trying out for a play, or a team sport? Don't you ever wish you could at least try it?" Danielle asked.

"I'd love to go out for girls' basketball," Haley said. "But I know I can't. It's part of being a skater. We all knew we'd have to give up a lot for it."

"Oh, I know," Danielle agreed. "But sometimes it bothers me, that's all. I mean, there are other things in life besides skating and homework."

"There are? What?" Haley joked. "Hey. Think about how great it is to get up at five o'clock every morning."

Danielle wanted her friends to understand what she meant. But it seemed they were having trouble understanding her feelings.

"But what if there's something you like even better than skating? If you never try anything else, how will you know?" Danielle asked.

"You mean, find something I like better than skating?" Nikki asked.

"Well, it is possible, isn't it?" Danielle asked.

"I don't know," Nikki said. "I can't imagine liking anything better than skating."

"There's nothing else I'd get up at five to do," Haley agreed.

"Anyway," Tori went on, "none of that other stuff is important. It doesn't get you anywhere. It's not at all like skating."

Before Danielle could respond, Kathy blew her whistle. "Let's get to work, girls. Warm-up's over."

Am I the only one who feels this way? Danielle wondered. Doesn't it ever bother them that skating takes up their whole lives?

4

A week later Danielle followed Megan into the *Grandview Gazette* office. She was nervous. Had they read her article? Was she welcome here? She wasn't even an official member of the staff.

Megan took her hand. "Come on, I'll introduce you to Sarah. She's the editor. Sarah Cohen, this is Danielle Panati."

"Oh, you wrote the skating article. It's fantastic," Sarah said.

"You liked it?" Danielle was relieved. She had worked so hard, staying up late revising and re-working until she believed the article was as good as she could get it. In fact, it seemed to be the only thing she had thought about lately.

"Liked it? We love it," Sarah went on with a smile. "It's going to be our lead feature for the sports issue." She looked around the room. "Do you know everyone?" She pointed to Ms. Howard, who was sitting at a desk with a pile of articles stacked in front of her. "Have you met Ms. Howard, our adviser?"

Ms. Howard looked up. "I know Danielle. She's one of my top students." She gave Danielle a big smile. "I'm so glad you decided to work on the newspaper. Your article is excellent."

Danielle felt great. She had been so worried that her article wouldn't be good enough.

"And this is Chip Mason," Sarah went on. "He's the sports editor. He's always looking for good writers."

"Yeah. It's tough finding writers who know sports, or sports people who can write. I try to avoid articles that say 'Ah, like, duh football team did good.' "

"Chip, that's unfair," Ms. Howard said. "There are several fine athletes who can write. Let's not stereotype people."

"I'm just kidding," he said. "Some of my best friends are football players."

"Okay. Let's get to work, everyone," Sarah said, calling the meeting to order.

Danielle sat with Megan. She listened intently as the staff talked about the design for the current issue. Then they began planning for the next issue.

"There's a dance recital coming up. I need someone to cover it. Anyone have any kind of background in dance?" Sarah asked.

Megan looked at Danielle. "Didn't you have to take dance lessons for skating?" she asked.

"Well, yeah, but I don't really know much. I mean, I'm not a very good dancer."

"Hey, you don't have to dance, you just have to write about it. How about it, Dani? If you've had even one lesson, you're ahead of anyone else in here. Right?"

"She's right, Danielle," Sarah agreed. "Can I put you down for the dance assignment?"

"Well, okay," Danielle said.

"Great," Sarah said, nodding. "Okay, next, an article on the Student Government Association elections."

The meeting ran on. Danielle looked at her watch and realized she was going to be late for skating practice. She whispered to Megan that she had to go. Then she grabbed her backpack and raced to the parking lot. Nikki was already waiting in her mother's car.

Danielle jumped into the car. "I'm really sorry," she said to Nikki and her mother.

"It's okay," Nikki said. "But where were you? I looked all over for you."

"In the newspaper office. At a meeting."

"Oh. Are you on the staff now?" Nikki asked.

"Well, sort of, I guess. I got another assignment."

"Really? But you just finished the one on skating. And you said it took forever."

"I know, but I really like writing for the paper. It's fun," Danielle said.

"Well, I've got enough work already," Nikki said. "Anyway, how will you have time to go to newspaper meetings and all? Those guys work pretty hard."

"I know, but I think I can fit it in. If not, well, at least I tried."

"Yeah, well, if I were you I wouldn't mention it to Mr. Weiler. You'll just get his lecture on how competitive skating demands total commitment."

Nikki had already changed into her skating clothes at school, but Danielle hadn't had time. As soon as they got to the rink, Danielle rushed to the locker room. Practice had started, and Danielle knew that Mr. Weiler would be looking for her. As she laced up her skates, she saw him frowning at the clock.

"Danielle," he said as she skated toward him. "This is the third time in a week you've been late for a lesson. What is going on?"

Nikki was right, Danielle thought. She couldn't tell him about the paper. He would never understand. "I—I'm just having some trouble with my schoolwork. I really have a lot this year," she told him.

"Try to plan ahead. Being on time is essential— as you know." He checked his clipboard. "All right, let's get to work. Let me see your double salchow."

Danielle was determined to get it right, but after a few tries she realized that today was not going to be any better. She still couldn't get the height she needed.

After several attempts, Mr. Weiler called a time-out. "How is your weight training program going?" he asked. "Is it helping?"

"Um, ah . . . ," Danielle began. He'd be furious if he learned she hadn't even started yet.

"What does Ernie say?"

"I, ah, I—"

"You are working with him, aren't you?" he demanded.

"Well, actually, he wasn't there last week when I went to—"

"Are you telling me you haven't started the weight program yet?" Mr. Weiler asked.

"Well, not really," Danielle answered softly.

Mr. Weiler sighed. "When do you start?"

"I don't know. I haven't talked to Ernie yet."

Mr. Weiler slammed down his clipboard. "Danielle. I told you two weeks ago—it is essential to strengthen your leg muscles. Two weeks. If you had been working out, your legs would already be stronger. Your jumps would be better. Do you not care?"

"I do, it's just that . . ." What could she say? How could she explain it? She didn't know why she hadn't talked to Ernie yet. She had been busy, but that alone wasn't an excuse. She just kept putting it off. She hated working out with weights, but that wasn't an excuse either. If she wanted to skate well, she had to do it.

He was watching her, waiting for an answer. Danielle just stood there, sliding her skates back and forth on the ice. Her thoughts were a confused jumble. She didn't know the answer. She looked up at Mr. Weiler, and suddenly the anger in his face was replaced by sympathy.

"Danielle," he began, "all skaters go through this sometimes. It's just a slump. You'll get through it. I'm sorry I got so angry." He put an arm around her shoulders. "You are very talented. It upsets me to see such talent go to waste. But it's natural to have a rough period. Don't worry. It will pass. For today, just take it easy. Work on your footwork routine, and try to enjoy it. Talk to Ernie as soon as you can. I don't want to pressure you, but strengthening those leg muscles is essential."

"I know. I'll talk to Ernie as soon as my lesson is over," she promised.

Mr. Weiler was right. She was in a slump. It happened to all professional athletes. It would pass. She began to skate a backward circle around the ring, trying to feel the joy she always felt in skating. She loved skating, she told herself. She always had and she always would.

5

Tuesday morning Danielle, Tori, and Nikki were in the locker room at the rink. They were just getting changed for school when Haley rocketed through the door. "There you are," she said when she saw Danielle. "Guess what Patrick just told me?"

"What?" Danielle asked as she pulled on a pair of jeans.

"Jordan wants to ask you out. He's going to call you tonight."

"Really? What if I don't want to go out with him?"

"What if he's madly in love with you? Patrick says all he talks about is how great you look now," Haley said.

"What nerve. Does he think I've got nothing to do but wait for him to call?" Danielle said. "I mean, he didn't bother to write or call all summer, and then just because I've grown a few inches, he decides he likes me again."

"So what are you going to say when he calls?" Tori asked.

"I don't know exactly, but I'm definitely not going to go out with him."

"You thought he was pretty nice the other day," Nikki commented.

"He was. But why go back to someone who dumped me like that? And anyway, I've kind of got my eye on someone else," Danielle admitted. She had been thinking about Zack Hutton a lot lately. She had seen him in the halls a couple of times since the first day of school, and he was always really friendly.

"Oh yeah? Like who?" Haley demanded.

"I don't think you know him. And anyway, it's no big thing. He probably doesn't even know I exist," Danielle said.

"Who? Now I'm dying of curiosity. You've got to tell us," Nikki insisted.

"None of you even know him. And anyway, it's nothing. I wish I hadn't said anything." Danielle pretended to study her hair.

Tori sighed. "Come on, Haley. It's almost eight. We're going to be late if we don't move it," she said.

"See you this afternoon," Danielle called to

Tori and Haley as they raced out of the locker room.

"We'd better hurry, too." Nikki stuffed her skating clothes into her bag.

As they left the locker room, it occurred to Danielle that she had to go to the dance recital that afternoon.

"Hey, I just remembered. I won't be at practice this afternoon. So don't wait for me." Danielle swung her skating bag over her shoulder.

"You won't? How come?" Nikki asked, surprised.

"I have to go to the dance recital," Danielle answered.

"The dance recital? Why?"

"For another article," Danielle explained. "I'm the only one on the newspaper staff who has any dance experience."

"You're on the staff?" Nikki cried. "I thought this was just one article."

"Well, they need new people . . . and . . . I like it," Danielle said.

"Can't someone else go and take notes or something?" Nikki asked. "I mean, it's not good to miss practice."

"Well, it's just one," Danielle said. "I'll make it up this weekend or something."

She pushed open the heavy metal doors that led out to the parking lot.

"There's Mom," Nikki said as Mrs. Simon pulled up in front of the building. Danielle and Nikki climbed into her car. They got to school before the early bell.

Danielle was hurrying to her locker when Mrs. Parsons, her history teacher, came over to her. "Great article, Danielle," Mrs. Parsons said. "I didn't know you wrote for the paper."

"Oh, is it out?" Danielle asked. "I haven't seen it yet."

"It's out and it's an excellent issue." Mrs. Parsons held out a copy of the paper. "Here. I picked up an extra one. Take a look."

Danielle had seen the final layout, but that wasn't the same as seeing the printed newspaper. Quickly she turned to the features section. There it was. Her article! Right there on the first page.

Danielle stared at her byline: "by Danielle Panati." She read it again and again. Seeing her name in black and white made her feel great. It looked like a name that belonged to someone important. Danielle Panati. Oh yes, the journalist.

She read her article over again, trying to imagine she was reading it for the first time, as her friends and teachers would be doing. Would the article interest them? She knew the words so well, she almost had them memorized. How would they sound to her friends and teachers?

"Danielle," Nikki called. Danielle quickly turned

the page, embarrassed to be caught reading her own article.

"Your article looks great. And the picture of Jill is terrific, isn't it?" Nikki said. There was a big photo of Jill beneath the headline "The Skating Life."

"Thanks. Yeah, Jill looks great. I hope she likes it."

The bell rang, and Nikki slammed her locker. "See you at lunch," she called.

Danielle had English second period. She couldn't wait to see what Ms. Howard would say about her article. Of course, she had already read it. But now that it was actually published, she was sure to say something new.

As Danielle stepped into her English classroom, Ms. Howard waved her issue of the paper. "Have you seen it? Isn't it fabulous? It's our best issue yet," she said happily. "I'm so glad you've joined us, Danielle." She put her arm around Danielle's shoulder and gave her a squeeze.

"Me too," Danielle said. She walked to her desk in a daze. Ms. Howard was the coolest teacher in school, and she had just given Danielle a hug. Danielle really was part of the newspaper staff now.

"Isn't it great?" Megan said as Danielle slid into the seat beside her. "Your article is the best."

All during English, Danielle tried to put the newspaper out of her mind. She tried to concentrate on the class discussion, but what she really wanted was to read the rest of paper right then. She wanted to see how everyone else's articles had turned out.

Finally class was over. Megan said, "What class do you have next? I've got a free period. I was going to go to the newspaper office. Want to come?"

"I can't," Danielle said. "I've got math."

"Oh, well, sit with me at lunch, okay? We can hash over the issue."

"Okay. See you then," Danielle said. She usually sat with Nikki and Jill, but she knew they would understand that today was special.

At lunch she found Megan sitting with Jessie Silverman, another girl on the newspaper staff.

"Sit here, Danielle," Jessie said, clearing a space where Danielle could put her lunch.

Danielle had just taken a bite of her turkey sandwich when Jill and Nikki came by. Danielle's mouth was full, but she waved for Jill to stop.

Before Danielle could say a word, Megan called, "Jill, how about the article? Do you like it?"

Jill stopped at their table, holding her tray of food. She wrinkled her nose. "The picture makes me look sort of nerdy. I mean, I'm standing holding my skates and staring at them like I've never seen a pair of ice skates before. It's a good article, though," she added quickly, looking at Danielle.

Danielle slid her chair over. "Sit here. Grab a

chair from that table. We can all fit." It was a table for four, and they weren't supposed to move the chairs to other tables, but sometimes they did it anyway.

Nikki looked around for a free chair. At that moment Danielle felt two hands on her shoulders. She looked up to see Chip Mason smiling down at her. He perched on the edge of Megan's chair and leaned next to Danielle. "About a million people have told me they loved your article," Chip said. "And no one's mentioned my soccer article. I think I'm jealous." He pulled three peanut butter and jelly sandwiches and an orange out of his lunch bag.

"I guess you like peanut butter and jelly, huh, Chip?" Megan asked.

He shrugged. "Not really, but I was in a hurry when I made my lunch. Look at this orange. It's ancient. It's hard. I think it's petrified."

Danielle smiled. Chip is funny, she thought. She would like to get to know him better.

"So what's the starting bid for this antique orange?" Chip said, waving it around.

"There's a special meeting tomorrow, you know," Megan said, ignoring Chip. "And a party afterwards." She pointed her straw at Danielle. "You have to be there. No excuses."

Danielle thought for a minute. Last period Thursday. She had study hall. She had planned to use it to work on her history paper, but she could go to the meeting instead. "I can make the meeting," she told them.

"What about the party? That's the important part," Chip said. He had finished his second sandwich and was unwrapping the third.

Danielle shook her head. "I can't. I've got skating practice. I have to miss it this afternoon because of the dance recital. I can't miss twice in one week."

"But you skate every morning, too, don't you?" Megan asked.

Danielle nodded. "From five-thirty to seven-thirty."

"Five-thirty?" Chip's eyes widened in horror. "You mean, like, in the morning?"

Danielle laughed at his expression.

"Skating at five-thirty in the morning. That's twisted," Chip added.

"You get used to it," Danielle said with a shrug.

"I really admire you guys," said Jessie. "I mean, it takes such dedication."

"You really have to love it," Danielle agreed.

"But don't you feel like you're missing out on other things sometimes?" Megan asked.

"Yeah, like sleep," Chip joked.

Megan rolled her eyes at him. "I mean, like being on teams, or in a play, or going to parties and stuff."

"Sometimes. But I really love skating," Dani said. Suddenly she remembered Nikki and Jill. They had been looking for extra chairs, and then they'd disappeared. She'd forgotten all about them!

She looked around and saw them sitting at their regular table, deep in conversation. Danielle felt a stab of guilt. She hadn't meant to snub her old friends for her new ones. Are they mad at me? she wondered.

6

Danielle was rushing out of English class when Ms. Howard called to her. "See you at the meeting later, Danielle. Can you stay for the party?" Today Ms. Howard's thick, curly brown hair was pulled back in a leather barrette. Some strands had escaped, and she twirled one around her finger as she spoke. "I made a batch of my famous fudge brownies. Actually, they came out of a box, but you won't tell anyone, will you?" She smiled at Danielle.

"Umm, I'll be there for the meeting but not for the party," Dani said. "I've got skating."

"Oh, yes. I'd forgotten that you're a skater as well as a writer. You know, when I read your article I was really struck by what you said—about the discipline and concentration it takes to be a top skater. A lot like writing, isn't it?"

"I never really thought about it before. I guess there are similarities," Danielle said.

"Well, if you find you can make the party, it'll be lots of fun. And if you can't make it, I'll save you a brownie."

"Thanks, Ms. Howard. See you later."

Later that afternoon, Danielle hurried down the hall to the newspaper office. She could hear the buzz of voices. As soon as she walked in the door, someone handed her an article to proofread.

Danielle proofed the article, marking a few typos and spelling errors. She handed it back.

Jessie handed her another article. "Read this over, would you? It's my editorial—why the Student Government Association needs more power. I have a feeling the article needs more power, too. I'm not sure what to do with it. See what you think."

Danielle settled down on the floor in a corner so that she could really concentrate. As she read she was impressed. Jessie's argument was clear, well supported, and convincing. There was just one paragraph that seemed weak. When Danielle finished reading she handed the article back to Jessie. "I think it's great," she said. "You really make your point."

Danielle wasn't sure if she should point out the one paragraph she didn't like. She didn't want to offend Jessie, and after all, Danielle was a newcomer. Jessie had much more experience on the newspaper than she did.

"Thanks. Any suggestions? I feel like it needs something."

"Well, there is one thing. This paragraph." Danielle pointed out the weak spot with her pencil. "It could be stronger. Maybe if you rework it . . ."

Jessie read it over, nodding. "Yeah, I see what you mean." She thought for a minute, nibbling on the end of her pencil. Then she scribbled some changes in the margin. "You think this works better?"

Danielle read over the changes. "Much better," she said. "It's really strong."

"Thanks, Danielle. That's just what it needed. Hey, you're a good editor."

Danielle noticed that lots of the other kids were exchanging articles and talking about changes. "Does everyone critique each other this way?" she asked.

"Pretty much," Jessie answered. "The editors don't have time to work on every article, so we all help out. A fresh pair of eyes, you know, that's really all it takes sometimes."

Danielle liked the way everyone worked together. It was so different from skating. There you were more on your own; everyone competed against everyone rather than helping each other out.

Work on the individual articles continued until Sarah rapped on the desk. "Okay, people," she said. "We need ideas for the upcoming issues. Turn your brains on and start thinking."

"Anyone got any food? I can't think unless I'm eating," Chip said.

"You can't think no matter what, Chip, so just sit there and pretend," Sarah teased.

"How about an article on the art department?" someone suggested. "Didn't some kid just win an art award?"

"I think we need an editorial about homework. The teachers need to coordinate so we don't end up with five tests on the same day," said a girl named Ellen.

"Yeah, everyone's complaining about it," said a guy Danielle didn't know.

"Okay. Anyone want to take it?" Sarah asked.

A few people raised their hands, and Sarah assigned the article to one of them.

They went on brainstorming until they had enough articles for the next issue and some ideas for the following one.

"Okay. Let's go over the schedule." Sarah flipped the calendar in front of her. "If we want the next issue to come out on the sixteenth, we'll need copy by Monday. Anyone got a problem with that?" she asked. "Danielle, how about the dance recital article? Can you get it to me by then?"

"Next Monday? I think so. It's coming along okay."

"Good. By the way, everyone loved the skating article," Sarah said. "You did a super job on it."

Danielle smiled. Sarah's praise felt great. Finally the meeting was over.

"Okay. Party time," Chip said. "Where's that CD player?"

Chip swung his baseball cap around backward. Jeffry Gaines flipped it off, placed it on his own head, and started rapping, "Yo dude we got da music, got da player, got the discs, yo dude we got da cookies, got da chips, got da food—"

"Yo dude, shut up before we lose da people," Chip rapped back, grabbing his hat.

Danielle laughed as loudly as everyone else.

Chip and Jeffry had the CD player set up in a few minutes. Soon rock music was blaring. Ms. Howard cleared off the big desk, and she, Megan, and Jessie put out brownies, cookies, soft drinks, chips, and dip.

Danielle began to pack up, wishing she could stay for the party.

"Hey, what are you doing? You can't leave. Parties are required. Right, Ms. Howard?" Chip said.

"I'm afraid Danielle has other commitments, Chip."

Danielle looked at the others. "I wish I could stay," she said, shoving her notebook into her backpack. "But like I told you yesterday, I have afternoon practice."

"Couldn't you make it up some other time?" Megan coaxed.

Danielle thought for a minute. "Actually, I could make up the practice this weekend." She smiled. "Maybe I will stay."

"My mom can give you a ride home after the party," Megan pointed out.

"Really?" Danielle asked. That way her parents might never even find out she had missed practice again.

"Sure. She has to pick me up anyway. It's no trouble."

"Well, okay. I'll tell Nikki to go without me. Be right back."

Danielle raced down the hall and out to the parking lot. Nikki was on her way to her mother's car, lugging her backpack and skating bag.

"Nikki," Danielle called, running toward her.

"Hey, Mom's here. Where's your stuff?" Nikki asked.

"Umm, listen." Danielle hesitated. "I'm not coming. I have to stay for the meeting."

"But this will be the second practice this week you've missed. Mr. Weiler's gonna go berserko." Nikki dropped her backpack, fished in her pocket for a scrunchie, and pulled her hair back. Then she hoisted the backpack onto her shoulder again.

"I know," Danielle said, "but I really want to stay. Tell him . . . tell him I'm flunking math and I have to be tutored. . . . Tell him—just tell him anything."

"Okay, but—" Nikki started. Then she slapped her forehead. "Darn. I forgot my math book. I've got to go back."

Nikki's homeroom was across the hall from the classroom the newspaper staff used. As they hurried down the hall, Danielle could hear music blaring and kids laughing and talking. The party was in full swing. And she knew Nikki could hear all the festivities, too.

Danielle stopped just outside the open door of the party. "Listen, I'll call you tonight," she told Nikki.

Nikki glanced toward the newspaper room. "Sounds like a fun meeting," she said. "Too good to miss, huh?"

At that moment, Chip ran out of the room and put his arm around Danielle's shoulders. "Here she is. She's staying."

Danielle saw Nikki shaking her head as Chip steered Danielle back into the party room and over to the CD player. "What do you want to hear?" he asked.

"First come eat!" Megan cut in. "Before the vultures finish it off." She pulled Danielle over to the desk. "There's a feeding frenzy going on here."

Chip quickly piled his paper plate with food. Danielle laughed. She knew Nikki disapproved of her behavior and that she'd pay for it tomorrow morning when she saw Mr. Weiler, but for now she was glad she had stayed for the party.

When the party was over, Megan's mother drove them home. Danielle climbed out of the car, swinging her backpack onto her shoulder. "Thanks, Mrs. McCord. Thanks, Megan. I'll see you tomorrow." As she closed the car door, Danielle saw her mother's car coming up the street.

She hurried up the walk and let herself in the front door. She hoped her mother hadn't noticed that she had come home with the McCords instead of with Nikki.

Danielle dumped her backpack in the hall and headed for the kitchen to get a snack. She heard the front door open. Her mother called, "Hi, honey."

"Hi, Mom," Danielle called back.

In a minute Mrs. Panati appeared in the kitchen. She dropped her briefcase and kicked off her high heels. "How was your day?" she asked, leaning across the counter and giving Danielle a kiss on the cheek. Mrs. Panati was a small woman, several inches shorter than Danielle.

"Okay," Danielle said cautiously. Her mother must not have noticed who Danielle had come home with. She breathed a small sigh of relief. But it was too soon.

"Whose car was that?" Mrs. Panati asked. "Not the Simons'."

"It was Megan McCord's, Mom," Danielle told her.

"Megan McCord?" Her mom looked puzzled. "She doesn't skate with you."

"I—uh—I didn't go to skating practice today."

"Was it canceled or something?" Her mother checked the pot of soup that was simmering on the stove. "Yum. Grandma's making minestrone for dinner."

"No, I—um—I had a meeting for the newspaper. It ran kind of late and I missed my ride."

Her mother spun around to look at her. "Nikki and Mrs. Simon left without you?"

"Well, not exactly. I sort of told them to go. I didn't want to miss the meeting."

Mrs. Panati stared at Danielle, wrinkling her forehead the way she did when she was confused. "You mean you chose to miss practice?" she asked.

"Yes, Mom," Danielle admitted. "I missed it on purpose."

Her mother shook her head as if she hadn't heard right. "You missed practice on purpose?" she repeated.

Danielle let out an exasperated sigh. "It's just skating practice, Mom. You're acting like I skipped two weeks of school."

"I'm surprised, that's all. This newspaper must mean a lot to you."

"It does. It really does. I—I just really like it. I want to keep doing it."

Her mother opened the refrigerator, grabbed a can of raspberry spritzer, and popped it open. She took a sip and reached across the counter to smooth Danielle's hair. "Well, I'm glad you like it so much, honey, but are you being realistic? I mean, skating takes up so much time, and with your homework . . ."

"I can handle it, Mom," Danielle assured her. "Don't worry."

"Just don't overdo it, sweetie. You tend to push yourself awfully hard."

Danielle had always pushed herself, both with skating and homework. But lately she hadn't been pushing her skating at all.

Well, she thought, that's what coaches are for, right? Mr. Weiler does enough pushing. The thought of Mr. Weiler made her frown. He was not going to be happy that she'd missed practice. Well, she'd deal with that tomorrow morning.

Right now she planned to work on the dance article.

Danielle and Megan sat at the counter in the Panatis' kitchen. They had a ton of proofreading to do for the newspaper. Danielle had to admit, though, that they were doing more talking than reading.

Danielle finished telling Megan about the girl whose locker was next to hers. "She complains just because I put my stuff in front of my locker. 'It doesn't fit inside,' I said, and she goes, 'Well if you'd clean it out, maybe it would.' So I said, 'Who are you, the locker police?' Can you believe that?"

At that moment Danielle's brother, Nicholas, came barreling through the kitchen door with his friend Zack. "Can you believe it, Zack?" Nicholas imitated Danielle. "I mean, really, can you believe it?"

Zack laughed. "It must be tough to have a brother like him," he said to Danielle.

"Tough? It's torture," Danielle said. She hadn't known Zack was visiting. She wished she was wearing her new sweater instead of the old sweatshirt she had on. She wondered if she should go up and change. Or would it be too obvious?

Nicholas grabbed two cans of Coke from the fridge. "Come on, Zack. Let's go up to my room."

But Zack sat down on a stool across the counter from Danielle and Megan. Zack was tall and thin, with curly brown hair that he kept kind of long. He wore a leather thong with three beads around his neck. He's so cute, Danielle thought, trying not to stare at him.

"Hey. I really liked the article you wrote for the last issue of the paper," he told Danielle.

"Thanks," Danielle said, wishing she could think of something witty to say.

"Is this the next issue?" Zack looked at the page proofs they had spread out on the counter.

"Yup. We're supposed to be proofreading, but we're not getting very far," Danielle told him.

Zack stood up. "Well, I guess we better let you get back to work, then," he said.

"Oh, I didn't mean because of you. It's just that we keep talking." Danielle blushed, wishing she had kept her mouth shut.

"Come on," Nicholas told Zack. "I want you to hear my new Pearl Jam CD."

"See you later, Danielle." Zack followed Nicholas out of the kitchen.

"Wow. He's cute," Megan said.

"I know. I think I have a crush on him," Danielle admitted.

"I think it's mutual. Did you see the way he looked at you?" Megan said.

"I don't know. He might just be friendly," Danielle said. But she hoped Megan was right.

"What do you think of Chip?" Megan asked.

"He's cute, too. And funny. Why? Do you like him?"

Megan nodded. "Kind of, but he's never paid much attention to me. I wish I could get him to notice me."

"Doesn't he have a girlfriend?" Danielle asked.

"Not that I know of," Megan said. "But I don't see him much outside of the paper."

"He was fun at the party," Danielle said.

"Yeah. It was a good party. Ms. Howard is so cool," Megan commented.

"And she's got great clothes," Danielle said.

"Did you see the skirt she had on today?" Megan sighed. "I'd kill for a skirt like that. But it would look awful on me. You have to be tall and thin to wear those. Like you, Danielle."

"Maybe, but by the time I get one they'll be out of style. My mom doesn't believe in 'trendy clothing.'"

"And I don't believe how much work we've got to do!" Megan said.

Danielle and Megan worked until eight forty-five, when Megan said she had to go. "I have to be home by nine." She gathered up her papers. "I haven't done a bit of homework. Have you started your short story for English yet?" She pulled on her jacket.

"I've started it, but I've got a long way to go," Danielle said.

"Me too. I'll be up late tonight. But at least I don't have to be up at five A.M—like you. I don't know how you do it."

Danielle wasn't sure how she was going to do it either. At nine o'clock she plopped down at her desk to begin her homework. She was just getting into writing her short story for Ms. Howard's class when the phone rang.

She picked it up and a familiar voice said, "Danielle?"

"Jordan," Danielle said. Last year when she heard his voice on the phone, her heart would start pounding and she would hardly be able to speak. But tonight she was irritated at the interruption.

"Um, I was wondering if you'd like to go to a movie next weekend."

"I'm kind of busy next weekend," Danielle told him. Why was he so interested now? She couldn't believe she'd ever had such a crush on him.

"Well, like, are you busy all weekend?" he asked. "Maybe we could do something Sunday afternoon?"

"I have to do homework then," Danielle told him. Maybe he'd get the hint and figure out she just didn't want to go out with him.

"Well, okay. I'll call you some other time, then."

"Okay," she said. Don't bother, she thought as she hung up.

After all the pain he had caused her last summer, it felt sort of good to blow him off.

She went back to her short story. It was about a girl in high school who was a fantastic ballet dancer. The girl's grandmother had also been a dancer. The girl was to perform in a production of *Swan Lake*, and the grandmother was determined to see her granddaughter dance. But the grandmother was very sick. Meanwhile, the girl thought she might quit the ballet because she no longer felt she could give it her all.

Involved in her story, Danielle lost track of time. When she finally looked at the clock she was shocked to see that it was almost one A.M. She put her story away and went to bed, falling asleep as soon as she lay down.

When her alarm rang the next morning, she felt

as if she had just turned out her light. Could it be time to get up already? If she could only sleep for just another hour. But she couldn't. She had to get to her lesson. She had already missed two practices too many.

Megan is so lucky. She has a few more hours to sleep, Danielle thought enviously as she dragged herself to the bathroom.

As she packed up her books she thought about her short story. She was pleased with the way it was turning out, but she needed to put more work into it. The ending just wasn't developing the right way.

Her mind was still on her story as she laced up her skates at the rink. But out on the ice, Mr. Weiler had his mind on her jumps.

"More height! You must get more height!" Mr. Weiler told her. "How is your work with Ernie going?" he asked.

"Fine," said Danielle. "I think it's going to help," she said, although she had only been to weight training once so far. It was so hard to find the time.

"Good. That is the key. We must strengthen those leg muscles to get the height you need." He nodded. "Okay. Let's try it again. This time pull your arms in sooner.

Danielle tried again, but in spite of Mr. Weiler's words, she forgot about pulling her arms in sooner.

"Danielle? Are you listening?" He skated toward her, took hold of her arms, and flapped them in and out. "Arms! Arms! Have you forgotten you have them?" Skating backward, he added, "Now try it again. And pay attention this time."

She tried again and again, but with no improvement. Finally Mr. Weiler held up a hand for her to stop. "Danielle, where are you this morning? Not here at the skating rink, that's for sure. You are a million miles away. Is something troubling you?"

"I was up late, that's all. I've got a lot of homework right now."

Mr. Weiler drummed his fingers on his clipboard. He seemed about to say something but changed his mind. "Okay. That's all for today."

She knew he was concerned about her, but she didn't know what she could tell him. She would work harder with Ernie, she decided, and really strengthen her leg muscles.

After practice Danielle went right to the weight room.

"Good to see you, Danielle. You really need to come regularly if we're going to strengthen up these toothpicks." Ernie showed her again how to use the leg lift machine. He adjusted the weight and stood back. "Okay. Let's try twenty reps. Go."

Danielle strained to raise her leg over and over. It was hard work. As she watched herself in the mirror, she thought about how fantastic her body looked. Her legs, once short and stubby, were now long and thin. Danielle didn't care what Ernie said about toothpicks; she loved being tall and thin.

Ernie had given her several sets of exercises to complete, but after only a few minutes Danielle wished she could stop. It was so boring! How was she going to make herself do this several times a week? She hated it, and besides, it hurt. Her leg muscles were killing her.

Danielle decided to switch from the weight machine to the stationary bike. At least she could watch television while she did that. She had just gotten on the bike when Jill came into the weight room.

"Danielle? Hi!" Jill peeled off her sweatshirt and positioned herself on a weight machine. "I'm glad you're here. Usually I'm all by myself."

"They've got me on a leg-strengthening program, so I'll be coming a lot," Danielle told her.

"Great." Jill hoisted the heavy weights with her legs. "It's more fun when you have someone to talk to."

"Fun! I call this torture." Danielle gasped as hot streaks of pain flashed through her thighs. She stopped pedaling and reset the bike to a lower speed. Beside her, Jill lifted a huge amount of weight over and over. "Wow. Your legs are really strong," Danielle said.

"They should be. I've been in here four times a

week for the past few months," Jill said, out of breath. "I can't wait to get back on the ice, and when I do I want to be ready."

"I can't lift nearly that much," Danielle said. "I guess I really do need to work on my leg strength."

"It's all I've been able to do since I hurt my ankle. I've lost so much time. I was such an idiot. One mistake, and look what it cost me." Jill wiped the sweat from her forehead with her sweatshirt.

"But only two more weeks, right? And then you're back on the ice?"

"Yup. I can't wait. It's been so hard. You can't imagine how hard. Sometimes I dream I'm skating and I wake up and realize I can't yet, and . . . well, I'm just glad it's only temporary."

Danielle watched as Jill did set after set of leg lifts. She had never seen such determination. That's what it takes, she thought. That's what it takes to be a champion.

8

Class was almost over, and Ms. Howard was finally handing back their short stories. Danielle had waited impatiently all period, but now she felt her stomach tighten. Ms. Howard placed her story facedown on her desk. She couldn't see the grade, and she was scared to look. She had put a lot of work into the story. She had liked writing it, but she had no idea whether or not it was any good. One minute she would read it over and think it was terrific and the next she would think it was awful. The story sat on the corner of her desk, daring her to turn it over.

"Aren't you going to look at your grade?" Megan whispered.

"I'm scared," Danielle admitted. "How'd you do?"

"B plus," Megan answered.

"That's great."

"Want me to look for you?" Megan offered.

"No. Here goes." Danielle grabbed the papers and flipped them over. "Excellent job, A. Please see me after class!" she read.

Danielle could feel her heart thumping in her chest. An A! It was a good story! All her effort had been worth it.

But why did Ms. Howard want to talk to her, she wondered? Danielle waited till most of the other kids had packed up their stuff and left. Finally, when the room was almost empty, she went up to Ms. Howard, who was sitting at the desk grading papers.

"Um, you said you wanted to see me?" Danielle said.

"Yes, Danielle," Ms. Howard said, smiling. "Your story was terrific. I enjoyed it so much."

"Well, thanks," Danielle said.

Ms. Howard leaned back in her chair and tilted her head to one side. "I was wondering how you'd feel about entering it in a contest?" She searched her desk drawer, riffled through some papers, and found what she was looking for.

"It's a contest for student writers, middle-school students. It seems to me that your story would be perfect. It would take a little revising, of course, but not a whole lot. I made a few comments you might want to look at, but you wouldn't have to do much work to get it ready for submission. What do you think?"

Danielle was too stunned to say anything. Ms. Howard actually thought her story was good enough to enter in a contest? Wow!

"You—you really think it's good enough?"

Ms. Howard nodded. "I really do. But it's up to you, of course."

"Well, yeah, yes. That would be great. I'd love to enter."

"Okay, good. Take the story home and look over my suggestions. If you have any questions, let me know. The deadline is the end of next week. Why don't you try to get it back to me by Friday? Can you do that?"

"By Friday."

"Good girl." Ms. Howard closed her notebook and glanced at her watch. "Uh-oh, I've got to hurry. I have a lunch meeting."

As Ms. Howard hurried out, Danielle slowly packed up her books. She was in a daze. Her story, in a contest. It was all she could think about.

She drifted down the hall to her locker. Luckily she had lunch next—she would have been late to any class.

Megan was waiting at her locker. "What did Ms. Howard want?" she asked.

"You won't believe this," Danielle said.

"What?" Megan looked closely at Danielle. "Are you okay? You look kind of . . . dazed."

"I am dazed. Ms. Howard just asked me to submit my story to a contest."

"You're kidding!" Megan cried. "That's fantastic. What kind of contest."

"A fiction contest for middle-schoolers," Danielle answered.

"Wow, Dani! That's so cool. And you were worried she wouldn't like it."

"I know. I can't believe it, can you?"

"I can believe it. You're a terrific writer." She grabbed Danielle's arm. "Hey, I've got to read this story. Can I?"

"I'm supposed to look over her suggestions and make some changes. I don't have another copy."

"Let's stop at the Xerox machine and make one."

On their way to the copy room, they ran into Nikki. "Have you eaten yet?" Nikki asked them.

"Nope. We're going to after we make a copy of Danielle's story," Megan told her. "Want to hear some great news?"

"What news?" Nikki asked.

"Ms. Howard wants to submit Danielle's story to a student writing contest," Megan explained. "Isn't that cool?"

"Wow. My friend the author." Nikki put her arm around Danielle and gave her a squeeze. "That's incredible. Ms. Howard is so great. You guys are lucky. I wish I had her instead of Mrs. Fishmouth." Nikki sucked in her cheeks, imitating her English teacher. Her name was Mrs. Fisher, but all the kids called her Mrs. Fishmouth.

"Hey, did you hear? Our next skating competition is in Philadelphia," Nikki said, suddenly serious.

"Yeah. It should be fun," Danielle agreed, though she couldn't really think about skating right now. She was too excited about her story. Besides, she knew she wasn't prepared for a skating competition. The thought that it was just four weeks away made her nervous.

"I can't wait. Philadelphia's so close to Seneca Hills, everyone will be able to come and watch us," Nikki went on. "You'll come, won't you Megan?"

"Definitely. I'll finally get to see what you guys spend so much time getting ready for."

Megan and Danielle stopped at the copy room. Nikki said, "I've got to meet Jill in the lunch line, but I'll save you both a seat. See you later."

Later that day at the rink, everyone was talking about the Philadelphia competition.

The minute Danielle stepped onto the ice, she could feel the buzz of excitement.

"All the local papers will be there. We may even get on TV," Haley was saying.

"My mother's already talked to a friend of hers

at Channel Five. She said they will definitely be filming us. She thinks she'll be able to set up an interview for me," Tori said.

"Cool. Can I be in it, too?" Haley asked. "I'll wear a really outrageous punk skating outfit. That way I'll be sure to get on TV."

As Danielle began warming up, she realized she didn't feel the same excitement that the others seemed to feel. All she could think about was how much she had to do between now and the competition. How hard she would have to work. She began skating her routine, hoping to lose herself in her skating the way she used to. Suddenly she remembered her short story. A thrill of happiness washed over her.

"Aren't you excited, Dani?" Tori asked when they took a break by the railing.

"I really am," Danielle answered. "Did Nikki tell you?"

"Nikki? No, Kathy announced it this morning," Tori said.

"Oh, you mean about the competition," Danielle said.

Tori gave her a strange look. "Of course. What did you think I meant?"

"I thought—oh, never mind." Tori would never understand. Danielle doubted the others would either. If she told them she was more excited about a short story contest than about the next skating competition, they would think she was crazy.

She looked at her watch and sighed. What was wrong with her? Practice had just started, and here she was counting the minutes until it was over.

9

When her alarm rang the next morning, Danielle heard rain drumming on the roof. It was a cold, dark morning, and Danielle felt groggy and achy. She burrowed sleepily into her bed, dreading the moment she would have to leave it. Maybe I'm coming down with something, she thought. She turned off the alarm, rolled over, and snuggled down into her covers.

Her mother knocked on her door a few minutes later.

"I think I'm getting a cold, Mom," Danielle called out. "I don't feel too well."

The bedroom door opened and her mother came in. She walked over to Danielle and put her hand on Danielle's forehead. "You don't seem to have a fever. Is your throat scratchy?"

"Kind of," Danielle mumbled.

"You'd better stay home, then. One day off won't hurt, and you don't want to get sick now. Go back to sleep, and we'll see how you are later."

The next time Danielle opened her eyes it was ten o'clock. The rain had stopped, and the sun was shining through her bedroom window. Danielle felt much better. I guess all I needed was to catch up on my sleep, she told herself. She climbed out of bed and began to dress. I might as well go to school, she decided. She felt fine, and she had a newspaper meeting last period that she didn't want to miss. She pulled on a pair of green corduroy pants and a navy pullover. She was brushing her hair when her grandmother peeked in at her.

"Oh, you're up. I thought you were sick," she said in surprise when she saw that Danielle was ready for school.

"I guess I was just tired. I slept until ten, and now I feel fine. I don't want to miss any more school. I can walk to school if Mom can't drive me."

Her grandmother felt Danielle's forehead. "Are you sure you're all right? A day in bed wouldn't hurt, you know."

"I feel fine, really, Grandma. I was just tired."

"Well, you have been doing an awful lot lately. Maybe it's too much for you, all this newspaper work on top of your skating."

"It is a lot, but . . . I love it. I don't want to give it up."

"Is it possible to do both?" her grandmother asked.

Danielle remembered her coach saying. "You'll have to give up a lot for a skating career. Other kids will be doing all kinds of things that you'll wish you could do, but it won't be possible. If you choose to skate, it will become your life. There won't be time for extracurricular activities."

"I—I don't know," Danielle admitted. "All I know is, I'm not willing to give up writing or the newspaper. I can't explain it. I just really love it."

Her grandmother didn't say anything for a minute. Finally she asked, "And what about your skating?"

"What do you mean?" Danielle asked.

"Do you still feel the same about it?"

Danielle said nothing. She sat on her bed, holding one sock. Her grandmother watched her, her dark eyes shining in spite of her age. Young eyes in an old face, Danielle thought.

"Do I still feel the same . . . about skating?" Danielle mumbled.

"Yes. Do you love it the way you used to?"

It was a question Danielle hadn't dared to ask herself. A question she was scared to answer. But her grandmother was waiting for an answer.

"I'm not sure anymore," she admitted. "I feel like it's work now. Something I have to do. Not something I look forward to, like I used to."

Her grandmother didn't seem shocked. Did she already know? Danielle wondered.

"But . . . but I can't quit now," she said. "Mom and Dad have invested so much money. And my coaches . . . Mr. Weiler would never understand. And my friends. What would they think?"

Her grandmother sat beside Danielle. She took her hand and stroked it gently.

"People change, dear. There's no law that says you have to like the same thing all your life. Why, what kind of a world would it be if we didn't change and grow?"

"Yes, but . . . I've put so much time into skating. And I'm good. I know I am. I don't want to just give it all up."

"As people get older, they face lots of choices. They're not always easy ones. The only thing I can tell you is this: It's a choice that only you can make. No one else can tell you what to do. You have to look inside, make this decision for yourself. Not for your family, or your coaches, or your friends. Only for yourself."

Danielle leaned her head against her grandmother's shoulder. Her grandmother combed Danielle's hair with her fingers. "I don't know what to do," Danielle whispered.

"Give it time, my dear. Give it some time."

At dinner that night Danielle and her family sat at the kitchen table. Nicholas was telling them about his hockey game. As he speared his third pork chop, he said, "You should see this new guy on our team. He's over six feet and has to weigh at least one-eighty. He's huge. And he can shoot!"

"Oh, I think Danielle has news, too," their grandmother said. "How is your short story coming, Danielle? Has Ms. Howard approved your revision?"

"She hasn't seen it yet. She needs it by tomorrow, so I'll have to finish it tonight. It's almost done."

"I'd love to read it."

"Okay, Gram. I'd like that."

"And what about the meeting? Were you able to make it today, dear?" her grandmother asked.

"Yes. And I'm really glad I went. Sarah, our editor, has been sick, and we're way behind schedule for the next issue. You should have seen us trying to do the layout without her. No one has a clue what we're doing. I hope she gets better soon."

"What's wrong with her? Nothing serious, I hope," her mother asked.

"Just a bad flu, I think. I'm sure she'll be better soon."

"I hear the next skating competition is going to be right in our own backyard," her father said. "I've already checked my calendar. I'm sure I'll get to see you skate this time."

"That's great, Dad." Danielle tried to sound more enthusiastic than she felt.

"I bet everyone at Silver Blades is pretty excited that it's going to be in Philly," Mr. Panati continued.

"Um-hmm," Danielle mumbled, looking down at her plate. She thought about her routine and sighed. She had so far to go. Would she be able to get it into shape for the competition? The thought that everyone she knew would be watching made it even worse.

"You don't seem very happy about it," her father commented. "I thought you'd be excited."

"It's just that I'm worried about my routine. I've got a lot of work to do between now and then."

"You'll do beautifully. You always do," he told her.

But there's always a first time, she thought. And then, before she really knew what she was thinking, a new thought crossed her mind. Maybe she wouldn't be skating in the competition.

But that was crazy. Of course she would skate. Why wouldn't she? She couldn't miss an important event like that. Her father was right; her routine would come together.

"Of course she will." Her grandmother echoed her father's words. "If she wants to, she'll do it."

10

The following Sunday afternoon, Danielle, Haley, Nikki, Tori, and Jill were sitting in a booth at Super Sundaes.

"I really hope we don't run into Jordan," Danielle said. "I told him I couldn't go out with him today because I had to do homework."

"That's the lamest excuse I ever heard. Don't tell me he bought it?" Haley said.

"I don't know."

"Even Jordan couldn't be that thick," Nikki put in.

"Why didn't you tell him the truth? That you don't want to go out with him?" said Tori.

"I didn't want to hurt his feelings," Danielle said.

"He didn't worry about your feelings this summer," said Nikki.

"I know, but . . ." Danielle took a bite of her ice cream. "You know how it is."

"So who's this mystery guy you have your eye on, Dani? You never told us," Haley said. "You know we'll worm it out of you sometime. So, you might as well just tell us and get it over with."

Danielle smiled. "I told you, you guys don't even know him."

"I know who it is," Nikki said. She leaned over and whispered to Jill. Danielle was pretty sure she heard her say "Chip."

Well, let them think it's him, she thought. That way they won't suspect it's Zack. She wasn't sure why she didn't want them to know. After all, Megan knew she liked Zack. But it was kind of fun having a secret from her friends. She decided she'd keep it to herself a while longer.

Anyway, she wasn't sure if Zack liked her. She hadn't seen him since the night he'd been at her house with Nicholas.

"Have you guys seen Alex's new haircut?" asked Nikki. "Doesn't he look dorky?"

"It is kind of short," Haley agreed.

"But he's still cute," Jill said. "And speaking of haircuts, I'm thinking of getting mine chopped."

"Really? Like how short? As short as Haley's?" asked Nikki.

"Maybe even shorter," Jill said.

"Hey, let's go to Cuts and Curls and look at the hairstyle magazines. We'll be your fashion consultants," Tori suggested.

"Cool idea," Jill said. "Maybe I'll get it cut today."

"Come on, Dani. Slurp down that sundae. Everyone else is done," Haley said. "Jill needs us."

"What would I do without you guys?" Jill asked.

What would any of us do without the others? Danielle wondered as the five of them linked arms and marched through the mall.

The following week Danielle worked hard on her routine. She ran through it again and again. By Thursday she knew she had it down. She had perfected the moves, but still there was something missing. She couldn't escape the feeling that she was just going through the motions. And it showed. She could tell. Her performance reminded her of a beautiful home that no one lived in. From the outside it looked perfect, but inside there was no warmth, no life. She wondered if she should talk to Mr. Weiler about it. But what could she say? How could she explain?

As she was cooling off, Mr. Weiler approached her. "Danielle, stop by my office when you get your skates off. I need to talk to you."

As Danielle unlaced her skates, Tori asked, "What does he want?"

"I don't know. Maybe it's about scheduling."

"Yeah, maybe," Tori said.

Danielle could tell that her friend didn't really believe it. She shrugged. "What else could it be?"

Tori frowned. "Well, you have missed a lot of practices lately."

Danielle pulled off her second skate and wiped the blades.

"But I've talked to him about that. He understands."

"Then it's probably no big deal," Tori said.

Danielle put her skates in her bag and stood up. "Well, here I go. Wish me luck."

She hurried down the hall to Mr. Weiler's office. She knew Tori was right. What Mr. Weiler wanted to talk to her about had nothing to do with scheduling.

Mr. Weiler's door was open, and Danielle peered inside. "Ah, Danielle. Come in," he said. He sat at his desk. Danielle took the seat on the other side of the desk.

Mr. Weiler put his fingertips together. He seemed to be thinking about what to say. Finally he began. "You have been working on your routine, and it is improving. Technically, it's quite good, but—"

"I know. It still needs work."

Mr. Weiler shook his head. "But, I am not sure that work alone will fix what is wrong with it," he finished slowly.

"What do you mean?"

"Danielle, a coach must be aware not only of an athlete's physical well-being, but of her emotional well-being as well."

Danielle nodded.

"I would not be doing my job if I didn't tell you what I see. What I see is that something is different. The spark that was once so compelling in your skating is gone. I watch you and I see that your moves are correct, but your performance, it's . . ." He seemed to struggle for the right words. He rubbed a hand over his face. "There's no feeling in your work. It doesn't come alive anymore." He folded his arms and leaned forward, looking at her intently. "Is something else wrong? Is there some problem at home, something that might be affecting your performance?"

His sandy eyebrows drew together over his blue eyes. Danielle knew he was worried. She didn't know what to say. She studied the nails on her right hand, wondering how to reassure him.

"It's important that you be honest with me, Danielle. I am your coach. I can't help you if I don't know the truth. You must tell me if something is wrong."

"Nothing's wrong, really," she told him. "It—it's just schoolwork. I have a lot this year, and math is really hard. . . ."

Mr. Weiler leaned back in his chair. "Danielle,

you have never had problems in school. You've been a straight-A student as long as I've known you. Are you telling me the truth?"

Danielle knew she couldn't lie to him anymore. He wanted to help her. If she kept the truth inside any longer, she would explode. Her eyes filled with tears.

At last she took a deep breath. "I just don't feel the same anymore," she blurted out. "I used to love coming to the rink. Practicing, working out. I loved everything to do with skating. But now, I don't know, it's drudgery. I keep thinking it will go away, that it's just a phase, but it hasn't. It just keeps getting worse. I . . . I don't know what to do."

Mr. Weiler waited for her to go on.

"I know there's something missing in my program. I know it's flat, but I can't seem to do anything about it. It's like I'm just going through the motions." Now that she had started talking, she couldn't seem to stop. "I've been thinking about quitting."

It was the first time she'd said it out loud, but she knew it was true. Maybe she had been thinking about quitting for a while without even realizing it. She wondered if her friends would understand. Quitting? It was the last thing any of them would think about. And was it really what she wanted? She didn't know.

She glanced at Mr. Weiler. What would he say?

Would he rant and rave and try to talk her out of it?

She expected to see shock and anger on his face. After all the hours he had put in working with her, even to think of quitting seemed horribly ungrateful. But instead of shock and anger, she saw sympathy.

"Oh, my dear Danielle—" he began.

"I'm sorry. I'm so sorry. I know it's awful of me. I don't know why I can't stick it out like the others, but . . ."

Mr. Weiler held up his hands. "No. You mustn't apologize. This is the way you feel. It's never wrong to face up to your true feelings. It would be wrong to pretend they weren't there, or to try to cover them up." He paused and sighed. "I won't tell you I'm not sad to see this happen. You are a talented skater. It's a pleasure to coach you. But these things happen, Danielle."

He picked up a pencil and tapped the notebook in front of him. "Still, this may be just a temporary slump. Maybe you need a short break. Some time away from the ice."

"Maybe," Danielle mumbled. By now tears were streaming down her face. But she felt better than she had in days. It was such a relief to be able to talk about her feelings.

Mr. Weiler handed her a box of tissues. "Do not be sad, Danielle. People get to a point where they no longer believe they can devote all their energies to skating. And then perhaps they *should* consider quitting."

Danielle shook her head in confusion as she wiped her eyes. "But how do you know? What if you make the wrong decision? All the time I've put in . . . And my friends. They'll never understand." She began crying again.

Mr. Weiler stood up, walked around the desk, and sat on the front corner. "Danielle, this is a very difficult decision to make. You don't have to make it all at once. You need time to think it over. To sort out your feelings."

"But what about the competition? I have to get ready."

"Your routine is technically excellent. A few days off won't hurt," he told her. "You must remember that no matter what happens, it is up to you. There is no shame in changing direction in your life. It happens to lots of people. Still, change is never easy. No one else can tell you what to do. Not me, not your family, and not your friends."

"It's funny. That's almost exactly what my grandmother said," Danielle told him.

"You don't get to be a grandmother without learning a little something along the way." Her coach smiled. "I'm glad you have her to advise you." He put a hand on her shoulder. "Take a few days off. Give it some thought. Maybe you just need a break."

Danielle stood up. "Thank you, Mr. Weiler. I feel much better now. I'll let you know what I decide."

"Very good, Danielle. Let me know if I can help, and remember, we've accomplished a lot, haven't we? You'll always have that, no matter what."

As she left his office Danielle felt better than she had in days. At least Mr. Weiler knew the truth. And he had been great about it. She hadn't been able to imagine how he would react. His calm acceptance of her feelings was not what she'd expected. What a relief!

She knew she looked awful. Her face was all puffy and her eyes were red from crying. She hurried to the locker room, hoping she could wash her face before she saw anyone.

But she found her friends waiting for her. "Dani? How'd it go?" Nikki asked. Then she looked at Danielle's face. "Uh-oh. Was he awful?" She held out a can of raspberry spritzer, Danielle's favorite drink. "Here. We thought you might need this."

Danielle took the can of soda. "Thanks, you guys." She wanted to tell them that Mr. Weiler hadn't yelled at her, but something stopped her. Could she tell them her real feelings? That she was actually thinking of quitting skating?

"Listen, Mr. Weiler's tough when he thinks

you've been slacking," Haley said. "He thinks we have nothing to do but skate. It's been so long since he was a kid, he probably doesn't remember what homework is."

"I remember once when I missed two practices in a row. Boy, did he let me have it," Jill added.

"And you have been missing a lot," Tori said. "You might need to rethink your priorities, Dani."

Danielle looked at Tori. That was exactly what she was doing, but she couldn't tell her friends yet. For them skating was the priority. It wouldn't occur to them that anything else might be more important.

"I know. I've really messed up lately," she told them. "But things are going to change. You'll see."

11

Danielle, Megan, and Chip sat at lunch with the page proofs of the latest newspaper spread in front of them. Megan handed Danielle's short story back to her. "I loved it. No wonder Ms. Howard wants to enter it in the contest. It's so good!"

"Thanks, Megan," Danielle said, taking the story from her. "It needs more work, but I'm really glad you liked it."

"So when do I get to read it?" Chip asked, offering her his potato chips.

Danielle almost choked. She looked at him wide-eyed, shaking her head while she swallowed a bite of her sandwich. When she could finally speak, she croaked, "Never! It's—I—you can't."

"But Megan says it's fantastic. I really want to read it," Chip insisted.

Danielle put down her sandwich. The thought of

him reading her story made her stomach knot up. "It's not that good. It's really kind of dumb."

"Oh, sure. Ms. Howard always chooses dumb stories to submit to important contests," he said sarcastically.

"Well, maybe you can read it sometime, but not now." Danielle spotted Nikki and Jill coming toward their table and waved to them, relieved to change the subject. "Nikki, Jill, over here," she called.

Nikki waved as she and Jill headed for Danielle's table. The relief Danielle felt quickly faded. How was she supposed to explain to her friends that she wasn't going to be at skating practice for a while? She still hadn't told them the truth about her conversation with Mr. Weiler. They had no idea she was taking time off to think about giving up skating. She knew she would have to explain it soon, but somehow she just couldn't bring herself to do it. Nikki was expecting her in the afternoon carpool, so she had to tell her something. But what?

"Proofreading, huh?" Jill asked, looking at the paper spread all over the table.

Megan nodded. "This issue is going to be super. Why don't you guys pull up some chairs," she said, folding up the proofs. "We're done with these for now. We can finish up later, right, Chip?"

"I'm done," he said. "Besides," he added with a mischievous smile, "I've got some reading to do." Before Danielle could stop him, he grabbed her story and dashed toward the door of the lunch-room.

Danielle screamed and raced after him. She couldn't let him read it. It was much to embarrassing. But though Danielle was fast on her feet, Chip was even faster. He quickly disappeared down the hall with her story.

Well, Danielle had to admit, a part of her wanted him to read it. But what if he hated it? What if he thought it was dumb? She told herself not to be so nervous. What difference did it make what Chip thought?

There was no point in worrying. She went back into the cafeteria to finish her lunch. Megan had left, taking the page proofs with her, but Nikki and Jill were still there.

"Chip is cute," Nikki said.

"And funny," Jill said.

"I can't believe he took my story. I really don't want him to read it."

"Why? I think it's nice that he wants to," Nikki said.

Danielle shrugged. "It's just kind of embarrassing. It's kind of like when someone who's never seen you skate before comes to watch you. You know how it makes you nervous?"

"Yeah, but that's different," Jill said. "I mean, Ms. Howard likes it. What difference does it make if Chip likes it or not?"

"Unless Chip is a very important person in your life," Nikki hinted. Just then the bell rang. "Uh-oh, we'd better hurry." Nikki piled her trash and dishes onto her tray.

"No, you guys don't get it." Danielle tried to explain. "It's not Chip that's so important, it's the writing. It really means a lot to me."

But Jill and Nikki were no longer listening. They grabbed their backpacks and started to leave the lunchroom. Nikki called, "See ya after school."

Danielle knew she had to tell Nikki about practice. "Wait," she cried. "I—I won't be coming to practice today."

"You won't? Why not?" Nikki stopped and stared at Danielle as if she couldn't believe her ears. "I thought Mr. Weiler was already furious about your missing so many practices."

Jill looked shocked, too. "Are you sure you can't make it? He's going to go bonkers if you miss another one. He just chewed you out yesterday."

"I already told him about it. I . . . It's a doctor's appointment," Danielle lied.

"Oh." Nikki looked concerned. "Is everything okay? You're not sick or anything, are you?"

"No. It's just a checkup, but my mom doesn't want me to miss it," Danielle said. She felt awful, lying to her friends. But they wouldn't understand. She knew they wouldn't.

All through her last-period class, Danielle thought how glad she was not to be going to practice. She was so excited to be working with her new friends on the newspaper instead. She hadn't realized she had begun to dread practice. The thought amazed her.

On her way to the newspaper office, she stopped at her locker. Nikki and Jill came by on their way to catch their ride to the rink.

"Should we be saying anything to Mr. Weiler?" Nikki asked.

Danielle shook her head. "I told you. He knows. You don't have to say anything."

"I'm surprised he let you get away with it," said Jill. "You know how he always says appointments should not interfere with practice."

Before Danielle could answer, Chip and Megan passed by. "Come on, Danielle," Chip called. "We've still got work to do on these proofs."

"I'll be right there," she told them.

Nikki and Jill looked at each other. "Oh . . . A doctor's appointment, huh?" Nikki said.

"Yeah. With Dr. Chip," said Jill. Nikki and Jill exchanged knowing glances and hurried away.

"You guys—wait!" Danielle shouted. But her friends left the school without looking back. Danielle stood in the hallway alone.

12

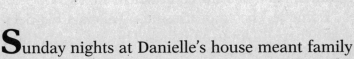

Sunday nights at Danielle's house meant family dinner. The whole family was supposed to be there, and they ate in the dining room instead of the kitchen.

It was usually a good time to talk about things that had bothered them during the week. Tonight, Danielle had decided, was when she would tell her parents that she was thinking about quitting skating.

She waited until they were almost finished. Then she said, "Mom, Dad, can I talk to you about something?"

"Hmm. Sounds serious," her father joked. "Let's see, you're not old enough to drive, so it can't be that you've wrecked the car. You just got a great report card, so it can't be about bad grades. What could it be?"

"Dad, this is serious," Danielle said.

"I'm sorry, honey." Her father put down his fork and leaned back in his chair. "Go ahead."

"I'm thinking about quitting skating."

Her father sat bolt upright in his chair. "You're what?"

"I said, I'm thinking of quitting skating," Danielle repeated, more quietly this time. Her stomach knotted. Nicholas stared at her in shock.

"Danielle," her mother said. "This is a big decision. There's a lot to consider. This isn't something you do on a whim."

"It certainly isn't," her father added. "After all the time you've put in—not to mention the money we've spent—you don't just quit all of a sudden."

"Wait a minute," Danielle protested. "I haven't definitely made up my mind yet. And it's not really all of a sudden. I—I haven't enjoyed skating for a while now."

"Well, that's news to me. Did you know anything about this?" Her father turned to Danielle's mother.

"I knew Danielle was having some difficulties because of her growth spurt. Franz mentioned it to me a while back. But he seemed to feel that all Danielle needed was to strengthen her leg muscles. You told me you were working with Ernie on that," her mother said, looking at Danielle.

"I was, but—"

"Danielle," her father cut in, "your body has changed a great deal in the past few months. It's going to take some time to get used to it. Naturally, it's going to affect your skating, but only temporarily. That's no reason to quit."

"It's this newspaper work, isn't it?" her mother said, shaking her head. "And your honors English class. It's too much for you. You're feeling overwhelmed. I'm sure if we can talk to your teachers . . ."

Danielle put her hands over her ears. Why couldn't they listen to her instead of lecturing?

"Wow," Nicholas said. "You're taking it worse than Dani."

"Perhaps you should hear her out," her grandmother said quietly.

"You're right, Mother. I'm sorry, Danielle." Her mother placed her hand over Danielle's. "I think we're ready to listen now. Why don't you explain how you've been feeling?"

Danielle's father nodded. "Go ahead, sweetheart."

"It's kind of hard to explain. I just don't feel the same about skating anymore. At first I thought it was just a slump. So did Mr. Weiler." Danielle shook her head. "But it didn't go away. It just kept getting worse. It's gotten so I dread practice. And I'm not the least bit excited about the competition."

"That certainly is a change. You used to live for skating competitions," her mother said.

"I know. But not anymore. Now I'm excited about the newspaper. About my writing. I just love it!" Danielle frowned. "I thought I could do both, but I kept missing practices. It just wasn't working."

"You always push yourself so hard, Danielle," said her father, reaching across the table to take her hand.

"But not with writing," Danielle said. "I don't have to push at all. I just like it. And the newspaper, too. I've met some great new kids, and Ms. Howard is so cool!"

"You certainly sound enthusiastic about it," her father said. "But have you talked to Mr. Weiler about all this?"

"He knew something was wrong. Finally he asked me what it was, and I told him I just don't feel the same anymore."

"What did he say?" asked her mother.

"At first he was upset, but then he was really great about it. He said people change and it's nothing to be ashamed of. He said I should take some time off and think about what I want to do. So that's what I'm doing."

"Well, that sounds like good advice. It's not something you should decide all at once," her father said.

"The thing is," Danielle went on, "I'm worried about all the money you and Mom have spent on my lessons. I know how expensive it's been. Now if I quit, it was all for nothing."

"All for nothing?" her mother exclaimed. "Oh, honey, don't be silly. Look at all you've learned. And I don't mean just about skating. It's given you so much. You've learned about competing, and discipline, and all kinds of important things. Things you can use your whole life. It's been a wonderful experience for you, no matter where you go from here."

"That's right, Danielle," her father added. "Your mother and I don't regret one penny we've spent on your skating."

"Hey, if she quits, we'll save a lot of money. So I guess that means I can get new hockey skates, right?" Nicholas asked.

Mr. Panati laughed. "We'll discuss that later."

"Dani, if you're taking time off this week, why don't we go shopping one afternoon?" her mother suggested. "You've outgrown all your winter clothes. We need to get you some new things."

And so Thursday afternoon, Danielle and her mother went to the mall.

"Isn't this fun?" her mother said, taking a sip of tea. They had stopped for a break and were sitting in a booth at the coffee shop. "We haven't had a chance to do this in ages."

It *was* fun, and they had found some great out-
fits. Danielle had forgotten how much she liked
shopping with her mother. Usually they were so
rushed they didn't have time to enjoy it.

"So. Do you miss skating?" her mother asked.
"It's a big adjustment. It must be hard to get used
to having so much free time."

"No." Danielle smiled. "I love it." She sipped her
milk shake. "It's funny, but I really don't miss skating at all. Right now, it's one big relief not to have
to go to practice. I . . . I guess I haven't enjoyed it
for a while, but I was afraid to admit it. I felt like
I was a failure or something."

Mrs. Panati reached across the table and took
Danielle's hand. "A failure?" She sounded shocked.
"Oh no, honey. You're not a failure. You've worked
so hard at your skating. You've given us moments
of real pride and pleasure, watching you. It's been
wonderful for all of us. But maybe now it's time
for you to move on. There's nothing wrong with
that. That's part of life."

"I think I know that now. But it took a while."

"Well, no wonder. It's a big decision. And sometimes it's hard to know what we really want. It's
hard to listen to yourself and not be influenced by
everyone else." Her mother put her cup down.
"How do your friends feel about this?"

Danielle felt her stomach tighten. She shook her
head. "I haven't told them. Not yet."

"But, honey, you have to."

"They'll never understand. Skating is everything to them. They'll think . . . I don't know. They might not want to be my friends anymore."

"You're afraid you'll lose them if you tell them the truth?"

"I guess I am afraid," Danielle admitted.

Her mother picked up her spoon and slowly stirred her tea, a thoughtful expression on her face. "You've all been friends for a long time. I'm not sure about this, but it seems to me that you have to trust them. If they choose not to be friends with you because your interests have changed, well, I guess that's a chance you have to take. But certainly they deserve to hear the truth. They may surprise you."

Danielle realized her mother was right. Now she just had to find the right time.

Nikki, Haley, Tori, and Jill had all called her during the week, but Danielle hadn't returned their calls. In school she had avoided Nikki and Jill. When she had run into them, she made up excuses to get away as quickly as she could. She knew they were hurt and confused. How would she ever face them now?

On Friday afternoon Danielle was in the girls' bathroom when she heard Nikki and Jill out in the hall. They're coming in here, she thought. Panicked, she dashed into a stall just as they opened the hall door. Danielle held her breath.

This is so stupid, she thought. I feel like a spy. I should just walk out and face them. She had started to do just that when she realized that they were talking about her. "I know," Jill was saying. "It's so pathetic. I can't believe she's messing up her whole skating career just because of a boy."

"Not to mention hurting her friends. The least she could do is be straight with us," Nikki added. "I tried to call her twice this week. She didn't even return my calls. It's like she doesn't even care about us anymore."

"She's really changed. Just because she has a crush on Chip and hangs out with all those smart kids from the newspaper doesn't mean she has to forget all about her old friends. I feel like I don't even know her anymore," Jill said.

"I'm not sure I *want* to know her anymore," Nikki added.

In a minute they were gone. Danielle was in shock. They were totally convinced she had a crush on Chip. She started to laugh, it was so funny. But then she stopped, remembering what else her friends had said. They were hurt. And angry. Danielle felt awful. But she couldn't blame them. How could they understand, when she hadn't been honest with them? What else where they to think? She realized it was all her fault. She should have told them she was thinking of quitting skating. The thing to do was to tell them the truth—and fast. She just hoped it wasn't too late. Giving up skating was one thing. She didn't want to give up her friends as well.

13

"**T**here you are, Danielle. I was hoping I'd find you before you left," Ms. Howard said.

Danielle was at her locker getting ready to go home. Ms. Howard handed her a flyer. "I forgot to give this to you after class today."

Danielle glanced at the flyer. "Student Writers' Conference." She felt a burst of excitement.

"I think you'll really enjoy it. And I particularly hope you can make it because they'll be announcing the winners of the short story contest there."

"I'd love to go," Danielle said. "It sounds great."

"Wonderful. I'll be going, and so will some of the kids from the newspaper. We can arrange a carpool. Of course, I know you have to clear it with your parents. Is the date good for you?"

Danielle read the flyer. Saturday, November 18. Her heart sank. November 18. The same day as the

Philadelphia competition. Oh no, she thought, then stopped herself.

If she wasn't skating . . . she could go.

"I'm not sure," Danielle said. "I'll let you know."

"Fine. Check with your parents and give me an answer next week. Have a good weekend, Danielle."

Suddenly Danielle knew. She would go to the writers' conference. She wouldn't skate in the Philadelphia competition. She was definitely going to quit skating—as of now.

She had made her decision. She wasn't going to change her mind—or regret it. She was giving up skating, and the time had come to tell her friends.

Had she waited too long? Maybe they were so mad they wouldn't even try to understand. Maybe they wouldn't want to be friends with her if she wasn't skating anymore. Would they see her as a quitter? A loser?

All these thoughts ran through Danielle's mind as her mother drove her to the rink the next day. Danielle was wearing jeans and a sweater. She didn't even have her skating bag with her. It felt strange to be going to the rink without her skating things. Of course, she knew that she would skate again, for fun if nothing else. But for now, she thought she should stay off the ice.

She had planned to arrive just as Saturday practice was ending. She would beg her friends to talk to her. They would listen. They just had to!

Her mother pulled up in front of the rink. She looked at Danielle with concern. "You're worried about what your friends will say, aren't you?" she asked, smoothing back Danielle's hair.

"I should have told them earlier. They're really mad at me now."

"I think they'll understand," her mother said. "Just explain that you've been confused. It definitely wasn't an easy decision to make."

"Thanks, Mom." Danielle gave her mother a kiss and slid out of the car.

She hurried toward the rink. It had been a week since she'd been there—the longest time she had been away from skating in years. Did I miss it? she asked herself. Am I fooling myself? How could I not miss something that has been such a big part of my life for so long?

People change, Mr. Weiler had said.

She was sure the time would come when she would miss it. When all her friends were skating in competitions and she was merely a spectator. But for now she was enjoying her new interests.

Danielle sat in the stands watching her friends out on the ice.

Nikki and Alex were putting the finishing touches on their routine. They looked great, moving together as if they were one.

Haley and Patrick were working on their death drop.

Even Jill was on the ice. She wasn't quite ready to compete in Philadelphia, but she was working on her jumps, and her ankle seemed to be holding up well.

As Tori executed a perfect double axel, Danielle felt the old pang of envy. She would never be able to do that now. But when she thought of the hours of work it took to get there, she breathed a sigh of relief that she didn't have to worry about it anymore. She could sit back and enjoy watching Tori do it, and not compare herself to anyone. The next time she went skating she would skate for pleasure. It would be such fun to enjoy what she could do and not worry about working on something new. Not worry about getting it absolutely perfect. What a relief that would be.

Nikki was the first to see her. She waved and skated over. "Danielle. Hi," she said, leaning against the barrier.

"Hi. You guys look great. This extra afternoon really paid off. Your routine is perfect. I know you're going to win in Philadelphia."

"Thanks." Nikki seemed unsure about what to say next. "Um—are you feeling better?"

Danielle blushed, remembering her lie about the doctor's appointment. She couldn't believe they hadn't really talked since then.

"Yes, I'm fine. But I've got to talk to you. And the others. I've got something big to tell you guys."

"Okay. Let's go to the snack bar."

Nikki clumped over to the bleachers and sat down on the bench to take her skates off. As the others joined them, Danielle told them the same thing.

"Is your cold better?" Tori asked. She sounded as if she didn't really believe that Danielle had been sick.

"Well, actually, I wasn't really that sick," Danielle confessed.

"I knew it," Tori blurted. "You didn't seem sick enough to stay off the ice. That was really dumb. You're going to be so far behind now. The competition is just three weeks away. How are you going to get ready?"

"I'll explain in a minute," Danielle said evenly.

Finally they were all settled at a table in the snack bar and everyone had something to drink. Danielle took a deep breath. "I know I've been acting really weird lately. I'm sorry. I . . . had a lot going on, and I didn't know how to handle it. I should have told you guys sooner, but I was so confused."

"Told us what?" asked Haley. "You're starting to scare me."

"Yeah. You're not moving or something, are you?" Nikki asked.

Danielle shook her head. "No." She took another deep breath, then continued. "But I am quitting skating."

For a minute no one said anything. They just looked at her as if they couldn't understand what she had just said. As if she were speaking a foreign language. "Quitting?" Haley said.

"Quitting," Danielle repeated.

"Forever?" asked Nikki.

"Well, I'll skate for pleasure, but not competitively."

"But why?" asked Jill.

How could she explain it? "I . . . I just don't feel the same about it. It's not fun anymore."

"But everyone feels like that sometimes. It's just a phase. It'll pass," Nikki assured her.

Jill agreed. "When I first got to the Ice Academy I thought about quitting. I didn't like it there, and it seemed everyone was so much better than me. But it passed."

Only Tori hadn't said anything. She was the last one Danielle had expected to understand. But for a minute Tori looked almost envious.

"Well," Tori said finally, "I think you're making a big mistake. Skating is not supposed to be fun. It's hard work, everyone knows that."

"But if you don't enjoy it . . . ," Nikki said thoughtfully. Danielle could tell she was trying to understand.

"Are you sure you're not just carried away by all the attention you're getting at the newspaper?" Haley asked.

"And by Chip. Giving up your skating career because of a boy—how dumb can you get?" Tori said.

"No. It's not that." Danielle had to smile. "This has nothing to do with Chip—or any other boy. I don't even like him. I mean, he's okay as a friend, but that's all. It's the newspaper I like."

Danielle glanced at Nikki. She seemed to be trying the hardest to understand. "Look, I know it's difficult for you guys to accept this," Danielle said. "I mean, skating's been our whole life. A few months ago I couldn't imagine my life without it. But this isn't something I just decided last week. I've been thinking about it for a while. I haven't been enjoying practice or competing. And the extra weight training was just the last straw. I couldn't face it. There are too many other things I want to do."

"Well," Nikki said slowly, "I guess lots of kids quit sometime. I mean, not everyone becomes a professional skater."

"But Danielle," Jill protested, "you're really good. You could outskate us all if you put your mind to it. It just seems like such a waste."

"I think you're making a big mistake," Tori said again. "You'll regret it soon."

"That's a chance I have to take," Danielle said.

"Tori, you should be happy. One less person to compete against," Haley joked.

"This isn't because of Mr. Weiler, is it?" Jill asked. "I mean, the way he yelled at you last week. Because you could switch coaches if that's the problem."

"No. And actually he didn't yell at me. He was really great," Danielle assured her.

"But you were crying and everything," Jill said.

"I know. Because I felt so sad—not because he yelled. Actually I think I knew then that I was going to quit. He told me to take time off and think it over. That's what I've done this week."

"Why didn't you tell us sooner?" Nikki asked.

"I should have. I know I haven't been honest, and I'm really sorry. But I didn't really know myself what I was going to do, and then I just couldn't tell you. I thought maybe . . ."

"Maybe what?" Jill demanded.

"Maybe you guys wouldn't want to be my friends anymore."

"Danielle, you should know better than that. There's more to our friendship than just skating," Nikki said.

"Yeah. And besides, if we weren't friends we might not get any more of your grandmother's cookies," Haley teased.

They all laughed. When their laughter died down, they were silent for a moment.

"I can't believe it," Nikki said. "You're actually quitting."

Jill reached out and took Danielle's hand. "I just wish you'd told us sooner. We didn't know what to think."

"I know. I'm sorry."

"You actually thought you could get rid of us that easily? Just by quitting skating? Ha. It'll take more than that to lose us, right, guys?"

"Definitely," Nikki piped up.

"You'll still come to Philadelphia, right?" Tori asked. "I mean, you can watch us even if you won't be skating."

"Actually, I can't make it this time," Danielle replied. "There's a writers' conference that Ms. Howard wants me to go to, so . . ."

"This writing really means a lot to you, huh?" Jill said.

"It does. It really does. I know this sounds crazy, but I love writing the way I used to love skating."

"That's cool," Haley said. "You're moving on. There's nothing wrong with that."

"That's true. Well, at least you don't have to worry about your routine for the Philadelphia competition anymore," said Nikki.

The subject changed to the competition. Danielle leaned back and watched her friends with a smile. They were her friends—they would always be her friends. She couldn't believe she had doubted that.

They were arguing about whose routine needed more work when Nikki glanced over at Danielle.

"Hey," she said. "Enough about skating. It's Saturday night. Let's get out of here and do something fun."

They left the snack bar and headed for the locker room, talking about whether to see a movie or go to the mall.

Just outside the locker room, Danielle said, "I don't have to change, so I'll meet you guys in the parking lot, okay?"

Danielle slipped out through the nearby metal doors of the arena. It was dusk, and a cold wind whipped her cheeks as she walked to the parking lot. She turned and looked back at the building where she had spent so many hours and collected so many memories. The sun had set, and the arena was a black silhouette against the red sky. As she stood there the memories came tumbling out, falling over each other in her mind.

She remembered her tryout for Silver Blades and how excited she had been when she heard the news that she had made it; the ice show in which she'd had the leading role; the exhilaration she had felt when she landed her first double axel; all the hard work, the hours of practice. She was saying good-bye to it all now, but there was so much that she was taking with her. She had gained self-confidence. She had learned so many lessons—about perseverance, about winning and losing. She would always have that, no matter what her future held.

A flash of light appeared in the black silhouette of the arena as the door opened and her friends spilled out.

"Danielle," they called.

She lifted her arm and waved. "Over here!"

"There she is," one of them said. They ran toward her and she was swept into their midst. The five of them linked arms and ran together through the cold night air.

Oksana Baiul is *so* graceful—she's like a ballerina on ice. And she can land the most amazing triple jumps! Oksana is from Ukraine, and she won the gold medal at the 1994 Olympics in Lillehammer, Norway.

The United States' **Kristi Yamaguchi** won everyone's heart when she took home the 1992 Olympic gold medal. But when Kristi was younger, she skated pairs! Here she is with her partner Rudy Galindo.

1992 and 1993 U.S. National pairs gold medalists
Calla Urbanski and **Rocky Marvel** perform an awe-
some death spiral. At Silver Blades, Nikki Simon and
Alex Beekman have been practicing their death spiral
so that it looks just as good!

Natalia Mishkutenok and **Arthur Dmitriev** from
Russia have great imagination on the ice. And Natalia
can twist her body into the most incredible positions!
Natalia and Arthur won the pairs gold medal at the
1992 Olympics in Albertville, France.

Everyone in Silver Blades wishes she could skate as powerfully as France's **Surya Bonaly**. She was the 1994 and 1995 World silver medalist—and you should see the amazing back flips she can do on the ice!

Elvis Stojko is so cool! He can really get a crowd rockin' with his great skating. Elvis is from Canada and is the 1994 and 1995 World Champion and the 1994 Olympic silver medalist.

At age thirteen **Michelle Kwan** was the youngest American skater ever to go to the Worlds! She's that good! She won a silver medal in the 1994 and 1995 U.S. Nationals and a gold medal in the 1994 World Junior Championships.

Kurt Browning always makes skating in front of an audience look easy. He's a great technical and artistic skater. I guess that's why he won the gold medal in the Worlds *three* times, in 1989, 1991, and 1992!

5

Jenni Meno and **Todd Sand** have the chemistry that makes pairs skating beautiful. They won a gold medal at the 1994 and 1995 U.S. Nationals and a bronze medal at the 1995 Worlds. As Silver Blades skater Haley Arthur always says: "They've got what it takes to be a perfect pair!"

Viktor Petrenko combined his athletic power and grace to win the 1992 Olympic gold medal. He's from Ukraine and has the same coach as Oksana Baiul. I wonder if their coach is as tough as the Silver Blades' coaches!

Brian Boitano won the gold medal for the United States at the 1988 Olympics. Today he's still competing and performing daring triple jumps and spins. Brian just gets better and better!

7

Nancy Kerrigan, the 1994 Olympic Silver medalist from the United States, skates with the grace of a princess. And she's a champion when it comes to difficult jumps and spins. Tori Carsen always says she loves the way Nancy skates—but everyone at Silver Blades thinks it's also Nancy's gorgeous skating dresses that Tori loves!

#4: Going for the Gold

It's a dream come true! Jill's going to the famous figure-skating center in Colorado. But the training is *much* tougher than Jill ever expected, and Kevin, a really cute skater at the school, has a plan that's sure to get her into *big* trouble. Could this be the end of Jill's skating career?

#5: The Perfect Pair

Nikki Simon and Alex Beekman are the perfect pair on the ice. But off the ice there's big trouble. Suddenly Alex is sending Nikki gifts and asking her out on dates. Nikki wants to be Alex's partner in pairs but not his girlfriend. Will she lose Alex when she tells him? Can Nikki's friends in Silver Blades find a way to save her friendship with Alex *and* her skating career?

#6: Skating Camp

Summer's here, and Jill Wong can't wait to join her best friends from Silver Blades at skating camp. It's going to be just like old times. But things have changed since Jill left Silver Blades to train at a famous ice academy. Tori and Danielle are spending all their time with another skater, Haley Arthur, and Nikki has a big secret that she won't share with anyone. Has Jill lost her best friends forever?

#7: The Ice Princess

Tori's favorite skating superstar, Elyse Taylor, is in town, and she's staying with Tori! When Elyse promises to teach Tori her famous spin, Tori's sure they'll become the best of friends. But Elyse isn't the sweet champion everyone thinks she is. And she's going to make problems for Tori!

#8: Rumors at the Rink

Haley can't believe it—Kathy Bart, her favorite coach in the whole world, is quitting Silver Blades! Haley's sure it's all her fault. Why didn't she listen when everyone told her to stop playing practical jokes on Kathy? With Kathy gone, Haley knows she'll never win the next big competition. She has to make Kathy change her mind—no matter what. But will Haley's secret plan work?

#9: Spring Break

Jill is home from the Ice Academy, and everyone is treating her like a star. She loves it! It's like a dream come true—especially when she meets cute, fifteen-year-old Ryan McKensey. He's so fun and cool—and he happens to be her number one fan! The only problem is that he doesn't understand what it takes to be a professional athlete. Jill doesn't want to ruin her chances with such a great guy. But will dating Ryan destroy her future as an Olympic skater?

#10: Center Ice

It's gold medal time for Tori—she just knows it! The next big competition is coming up, and Tori has a winning routine. Now all she needs is that fabulous skating dress her mother promised her! But Mrs. Carsen doesn't seem to be interested in Tori's skating anymore—not since she started dating a new man in town. When Mrs. Carsen tells Tori she's not going to the competition, Tori decides enough is enough! She has a plan that will change everything—forever!